Praise for *No Diving Allowed*

"How fitting the stories in Lou̲ ̲ ̲ ̲ ̲ ̲,
No Diving Allowed, feature swimmi̲ ̲ ̲ ̲ ...ters can
wade so far into the turbulent wate̲ ...my life. From suburban
Connecticut to the plains of Africa, Marburg offers shimmering,
iridescent tales of marriage, parenting, friendship and adolescent
discovery that capture the very essence of the human spirit. Her
pools are never still, but always run deep. John Cheever built a rep-
utation upon one breath-stopping swimming story; Louise Marburg
serves up fourteen. *No Diving Allowed* offers a penetrating explora-
tion of our emotional tides. Readers will be very glad to have taken
the plunge."

—Jacob M. Appel, author of *Millard Salter's Last Day*

"In her latest collection, *No Diving Allowed,* Louise Marburg's master-
ful prose shimmers and delights. Startlingly perceptive, these stories
plumb the depths of uncomfortable, half-understood emotions,
exposing her characters' unique vulnerabilities and exploring their
inspiring resiliency."

—Chris Cander, author of *The Weight of a Piano*

No Diving Allowed

Louise Marburg

Regal House Publishing

Published by
Regal House Publishing, LLC
Raleigh, NC 27612
All rights reserved

ISBN -13 (paperback): 9781646030774
ISBN -13 (epub): 9781646031023
Library of Congress Control Number: 9781646030774

Interior and cover design by Lafayette & Greene
Cover images © by C.B. Royal

Regal House Publishing, LLC
https://regalhousepublishing.com

The following is a work of fiction created by the author. All names, individuals, characters, places, items, brands, events, etc. were either the product of the author or were used fictitiously. Any name, place, event, person, brand, or item, current or past, is entirely coincidental.

Printed in the United States of America

For Charlie, always.

Contents

Identical

The summer before my final year of college, my uncle killed himself. He was out of his mind, of course, you'd have to be to put a gun in your mouth, but nobody knew it, he'd seemed happy enough. If my twin brother had killed himself instead of my uncle, people would have understood. My brother had attempted suicide the month before and had been locked up in a mental hospital since then. I thought my brother was a pain in the ass; he'd always been horrible to me. He could have stayed in the hospital forever and I wouldn't have cared, but they let him out for my uncle's funeral.

"Shut up," was the first thing Harry said to me when he walked through the front door with my parents. He looked bewildered, glassy-eyed. Like a convict just released from prison, he had on the same ratty tweed overcoat and filthy jeans he'd worn when he checked into the hospital. No one would mistake us for each other now: he'd shaved off his hair a couple of months ago and only about an inch had grown back.

"He looks like hell," I said to my mother. I made a point of talking about Harry as if he weren't there. I had argued against letting him go to the funeral, but my parents thought it would be good for him to see what killing yourself really meant. Apparently, he was too fucked-up or too stupid to realize it meant you were dead. He had tried to hang himself with his tie from a hook in the ceiling of the back porch, but the hook was meant for hanging baskets of flowers and the weight of his body yanked it out. Breaking my policy, I'd spoken directly to him when I told him the next time he tried to kill himself to do some research and get it right.

The funeral was at a nearby church that Uncle Fred had never attended, so the minister didn't have anything to say about him beyond a few nonspecific lamentations. Six of Uncle

Fred's friends carried his coffin, and his grown daughter, who lived up in Hartford, and my father, his brother, both got up and recounted moments in Uncle Fred's life with humor and pathos. Because Uncle Fred wasn't married at the time, the reception after the service was at my parents' house. It was June, and the weather was as good as it gets, warm in the sun, cool in the shade, the grass so thick and green it almost looked fake. There was a bar, and a bartender, and a buffet table heaped with hors d'oeuvres, and everyone stood around the sparkling swimming pool gradually feeling more cheerful.

My brother sidled up to me as I stood at the bar waiting for my second gin and tonic. The bartender handed it over and asked Harry what he wanted.

"Scotch, neat," he said. He sounded exactly like our father.

"Excuse me," I said, leaning toward the bartender and speaking *sotto voce*. "My brother is mentally ill and shouldn't mix alcohol with his antipsychotic." The bartender raised his eyebrows at me and looked over at Harry.

"He's joking, of course," Harry said.

"Whatever," the bartender said. He poured a couple of fingers of scotch and gave the glass to Harry. My mother's sister approached us.

"Harry, darling, how are you feeling?" she said, over-enunciating the words as if Harry were hard of hearing.

"Fine," Harry said. In fact, I had to admit he seemed fine. His eyes had lost their creepy sheen, and he'd put on a seersucker suit and an excess of lime cologne. "I'm interviewing for a job tomorrow. Just for the summer, until I go back to college."

"He's not going back to college," I said. "He isn't getting a job."

"I'm thinking of applying to law school when I graduate," he said. I wondered if he was hallucinating.

"Following in your father's footsteps?" my aunt said. She shot me a frantic look. It was common knowledge that Harry had dropped out of college in his sophomore year and hadn't held a job for more than a few months since then. "Well, I think that's marvelous, Harry. I hope you have a wonderful summer."

"A real chip off the block," I said as my aunt tottered away. I was the one who would be going to law school; I was working for our father that summer.

"Shut up," Harry said. My silence was clearly on his mind. I was watching a girl I wanted to talk to, waiting for a guy who was a well-known bore to move on and give me a chance. When he did, I hustled over.

"Claire," I said.

"Barry," she said.

"How's life treating you?" I pretty much knew the answer to that from stalking her on Facebook. She had one thousand fifty-six "friends," and, judging from her feed, partied regularly with a good portion of them. I had been dreaming of fucking Claire since eleventh grade, when I met her at a school mixer. She was two years younger than me, fourteen to my sixteen, but even at that age she shimmered with a pristine loveliness that immediately and forever became my notion of "sexy." I had jerked off to the image of Claire in my mind hundreds, maybe thousands of times. Naturally, she had a boyfriend, and then another after him, then another, and another, and another, a daisy chain of handsome guys that never seemed to break. But Claire's current boyfriend was volunteering for three months in a slum in Guatemala, a fact I knew from talking to her brother. Even if I couldn't steal Claire outright from this guy, I thought I might borrow her for the summer.

"So, how was Cancun?" I said. "Your Instagram photos were amazing."

"Harry, how *are* you?" she said, looking past my ear. "I'm so glad you're here!" Harry stood sheepishly a few steps behind me. I was surprised I hadn't felt him there.

"I'm great," he said. He dug his hands into his pants pockets. "You look gorgeous, Claire."

"You're sweet to say so," Claire said.

"He's only out of the hospital for Uncle Fred's funeral," I said.

Her lovely face crumpled, and tears welled in her delft blue eyes. "It's so tragic," she said. For a moment I was confused.

Was she talking about Fred or Harry? "Did you love him very much?"

"Uncle Fred? Of course," I said, though I hadn't really, or at least not much. He had been somewhat of a dick to me, and to a lot of other people, including his four ex-wives.

"What would make him do such a thing?" she said.

"I guess he was fed up with life." I could see that was the wrong thing to say by the perplexed expression on Claire's face, so I changed my tack. "He had seemed unhappy," I said in a grave voice. "But we didn't know what about."

"Some people are just more sensitive than others." She looked pointedly at Harry. Harry grinned and stepped forward like he'd been chosen for a team. "You're not that way," she said to me.

"Actually, I'm very sensitive," I said. I ducked my head as if overcome by my own sensitivity. When I looked up, she was gazing at the swimming pool.

"Summer's here," she said dreamily. "Doesn't the pool look delicious?"

"Why don't you come over for a swim tomorrow?" Harry said.

"I'd love to!" Claire said. "What time?"

Before I could speak, Harry said, "How about two o'clock?"

"He won't be here then, but I will," I said.

"He doesn't know what he's talking about," Harry said.

Claire smiled at us, first at Harry, then at me. "I forgot how hilarious you guys can be," she said. "Barry and Harry. I always thought it would be fun to be an identical twin."

"Oh yeah, it's a laugh riot," I said, and watched my sarcasm sail over her pretty blonde head.

I woke in the gravel-colored light of early dawn unable to take a breath. Harry was straddling my waist, his hands around my throat. I reached up and jabbed my fingers into his eyes. His grip on my neck loosened. I punched him in the nose. When he fell to the floor beside my bed, I slammed my foot down on the side of his head. Silently, he squirmed as I ground his ear into the carpet. When I finally decided to lift my foot, he scurried out of my room. He wasn't as strong as he used to be. He hadn't tried to hurt me in a couple of years, since he'd become more interested in hurting himself, and I wondered what had happened to remind him of his old habit.

"Harry tried to strangle me," I told my mother at breakfast. He was sitting across from me, a rime of blood in one nostril, eating a bowl of Cheerios.

My mother sighed. She was still in her bathrobe, a pilly old thing she'd worn since I was in high school. Her graying brown curls were flattened on one side of her head and frizzy on the other. Doubtless she was nursing a hangover; I certainly was. The reception after the service had gone unexpectedly late and gotten rowdy toward the end. "Honestly, you two. When are you going to grow out of these silly shenanigans?"

"Ask him," I said. "I have a right to defend myself. When are you taking him back to the hospital?"

"We're not," my mother said.

"Honey, I'm home," Harry sang. His voice grated on my ears.

"What?" I said to my mother.

"I told you we were bringing him home," my mother said.

"I thought you meant just for the funeral."

"I'm perfectly all right," Harry said through a mouthful of Cheerios. Again, I had to admit he did seem all right. He'd showered and shaved and was wearing a freshly pressed shirt.

"I wouldn't call attempted murder the act of a sane person," I said to my mother. "Attempted suicide, attempted murder; I'm seeing a pattern here. What will he attempt to do next, rob a bank?"

"Good idea," Harry said. "I could use the attempted money."

After breakfast, I drove to the club with my father for our weekly tennis game. The morning was dewy and cool, and there were only a few players on the courts. As I unzipped my racket from its sleeve, I felt my chest expand with the anticipation and delight I'd felt at the start of every summer since first grade. No school for three months was manna from heaven.

"I'll be easy on you today," I kidded my father. He used to beat me at tennis, but lately I'd begun to beat him. He sat on a bench at the edge of the court, the freckled bald spot on the top of his head reflecting the morning light. He looked glum, and I wondered why until I remembered his brother had just died. "You okay, Dad?"

He patted the vacant side of the bench. "Sit with your old man." When I sat down, he said, "You know your uncle and I weren't the best of friends, but I knew I could depend on him if I was truly in need."

"Did you really?" I said. I found this hard to believe. Uncle Fred had been famously selfish. I had never received a gift from him, for instance, and he was my godfather as well as my uncle.

"Yes," my father said. "Because no matter what, we were brothers."

"Ah." I could see where this was going and was determined to head it off. "Harry tried to strangle me this morning," I said. "Do you really think I can depend on him?"

"Listen," he said urgently. The tension in his face was a little bit frightening, though he was the kindest man I knew. "Harry will never be like other people; he's been...unusual...since he was a child. I understand you don't get along, but someday your mother and I will be gone, and you boys are going to be all each other has."

"No, we won't because *he* won't have *me* at all," I said. "I plan on moving somewhere very far away as soon as I finish college." That wasn't true, but the sentiment was. When I was on my own, I wouldn't ever have to see Harry.

"I hear you," my father said, which was what he always said when he was about to voice his disagreement. Of course he heard me; he wasn't deaf. "Life without family is lonely and unnatural. Though you don't realize it now, there is nothing more sacred than the bond of blood. Harry's doctor says it was only a matter of finding the right medication for him, and I think he seems well now. Better than ever. I got him an interview this morning for a summer job down at the boatyard, and he says he wants to go back to college. I doubt he'll ever live a conventional life, but he'll be a functioning member of society."

It had been so long since Harry was functional that I wasn't sure how I felt about it. I realized that his trying to strangle me that morning was a sign that he was himself again, and that he had in fact been telling the truth about the summer job was proof of a basic level of sanity. A man and a woman walked onto the adjacent court. The *thwock-thwock* of their lazy warm-up play made me happy about summer again.

"I have other family," I said. "There's Diana and Astrid and Jim." Diana was Uncle Fred's daughter, and Astrid and Jim were my mother's niece and nephew. I mentioned a few second cousins, one of whom lived in Nairobi.

"For pity's sake, Barry," my father said. "I don't understand your attitude. You and Harry share the same DNA. When you look in the mirror you see Harry's face, and the same is true for him. Turning your back on Harry is like turning your back on yourself!"

I couldn't fathom the stupidity of this idea. "Okay, so by your logic, when Harry tries to murder me, it's like he's trying to murder himself?"

"I don't know when you two will stop your foolishness," my father said. "Grow up. It's ridiculous."

I stood and bounced a tennis ball against my upturned racket, then caught it in my hand. I imagined carting Harry around in a sack on my back, bowed by his awful weight. I tossed the tennis ball to my father.

"Come on, let's play."

"Think about what I've said, will you?" he said.

I wasn't going to think about it. I was forgetting it already.

My mother set the table for lunch on the porch where Harry had attempted to take his life. The old metal hook he'd used to hang himself had been replaced by a shiny new one, and four baskets of petunias hung around the porch's perimeter as they always had. The porch was a pleasant place, striped with sunlight and shadow; it had a view of the swimming pool and wide back lawn, and occasionally a finch or sparrow flew in and perched inquisitively on the back of a chair. I wondered what Harry was thinking as we sat down to eat. He didn't look at the new hook, though he didn't appear to be not looking at it either. He put his napkin in his lap and buttered his bread. My mother served him some salad. My father wondered if anyone wanted wine. My mother and I said no, Harry said yes. My father got up to get it.

"They say alcohol is a depressant," I said to my father. "Do you really think he should be having any?"

"Harry, what does Dr. Greer say about alcohol?" my father said.

"I had several scotches yesterday," Harry said. "And I'm less hungover than all of you."

"Well, never mind about the wine," my mother said to my father, and he sat down again. I dug into my salad, navigating through globs of goat cheese and shards of almonds, red berries, and a nasturtium flower. My mother could never be satisfied with just putting lettuce in a bowl.

As I looked up to compliment her—the salad was odd, but delicious—Harry flung his silver butter knife straight at my head. The knife was heavy and had a centimeter of serration along its edge. It hit me in the forehead and fell with a clang against my plate, then to the floor between my feet.

"Ouch, goddamn it," I said as I felt my forehead. There was blood on my forefinger. I held it up for all to see. "Look, he can't even sit at a table for five minutes without being violent."

"It's just a scratch," my mother said as she examined my forehead. She turned to Harry. "Why on earth did you do that, Harry?" She sounded more curious than angry, which made me mad.

"Because he's insane!" I said. "He should be locked up."

"Because you're an asshole," Harry said. "You always have been. I can't wait until I never have to see you again."

"I actually dream about getting away from you forever," I said. "You've been tormenting me all my life."

"That's because you've been a tool since birth," Harry said. "Think about it a minute. Does anyone really like you?"

"Yes, people like me," I said through my teeth. It was true that I was never as popular as Harry growing up, but I'd had plenty of my own friends. I noticed our parents staring at us.

"You're speaking to each other," my mother said.

Harry laughed. "However nastily."

My father banged his fist so hard on the table that the china and silverware rattled. My mother and Harry and I looked furtively at each other.

"My brother just died!" he bellowed. "He killed himself and I have no idea why. I hardly knew anything about him, and now I wish I had. Maybe if I'd been there for him, he'd be alive today. Regret!" He stared at me for too long. "Regret is a terrible thing."

"But, darling," my mother said. "Fred was impossible."

"So what?" my father said. "He was my only brother. I should have made more of an effort." He pointed at me and then at Harry. "You two are as alike as human beings can be, yet you wouldn't lift a finger for one another, would you? You're a tragedy, the two of you! You make me ashamed."

I could hear the low hum of the pool filter through the silence that followed. I had no idea why Harry had tried to kill himself, and I hadn't wondered about it either. I looked at him. He was gazing out at the lawn. I hadn't asked him a question in years.

A voice came from inside the house. "Hello? Anybody home?"

"Out here," Harry called.

Claire came out to the porch. Harry and I stood up. My mother began clearing the table; my father sat in furrowed contemplation, his fingers forming a steeple under his chin. The straps of Claire's bathing suit peeked from her sleeveless pink shift, two brilliant stripes of peacock blue pressing into her creamy shoulders. Her golden hair was done up in a complicated braid that began at the crown of her head and was punctuated at its end by a fluttering ribbon that more or less matched her dress. Her toenails were painted candy-apple red. I imagined they would taste like sugar if I took them into my mouth.

"I like your trunks," she said to Harry. Harry was wearing a pair of swimming trunks that were printed with a pattern of interlocking red fish. They were mine, pilfered from my room, and I could tell Harry knew I'd noticed them by the covert glee on his face.

"Be right back," I said. I ran upstairs and put on a pair of navy-blue trunks that weren't nearly as nice as the ones Harry pinched. Chatter floated through the open window. I looked out and saw Claire and Harry standing by the pool. Harry made a wide gesture with his arms as if describing a very fat person; Claire laughed so hard she bent at the waist and clapped her hands over her knees. She tested the temperature of the pool with one foot and stepped back with a little squeal. Harry pretended he was going to push her in. *Again* she laughed—how was that at all funny? Then she pulled her shift over her head, and the peacock-blue bathing suit, a bikini, was revealed.

I ran downstairs and out to the pool.

"Oh, Barry," Claire said. She'd put on sunglasses with neon green frames. "Will you be coming to the opera too?"

"What do you mean?" I said.

"Barry doesn't care for the opera," Harry said. "Anyway, I only have two tickets."

"He doesn't have tickets to the opera," I said to Claire.

"I ordered the tickets online," Harry said. "The seats are pretty good."

Claire took off her sunglasses and looked suspiciously at me. "Are you guys fighting or something?"

"Of course not," we both said at the same time. I smiled at Claire; she was looking at Harry. He was grinning like an elf at Christmas.

"I've never been to the opera," Claire said.

"Neither has Harry," I said.

"You'll love it," Harry told her. "We can have a late dinner afterward."

A shrill whistling sound came and went in my ears, and the back of my throat felt thick. My upper lip was stuck to my teeth. A pulse banged behind my eyes.

"You're a shit, Harry," I said.

"You'll have to excuse Barry," Harry said to Claire. "A lady is present," he scolded me.

As if he already possessed her, Harry put his hand on Claire's shoulder. *Fine, take her,* I thought. Inevitably, I was the loser as long as he was around, banned from the clubhouse, pushed out of the tree. He stole my first crush, Mary Lannan, and he hadn't even liked her. I doubted he cared much, or as much as I did, about Claire.

My head felt like it was cracking apart. I covered my eyes with my hands.

"Barry, what's wrong?" Claire said.

I took my hands away. "I'm just tired."

"Poor Barry," Harry said. "Maybe you should go lie down."

"I am going to fucking kill you," I said. I locked my arms around him and flung us violently into the pool. We flew through the air, crashed into the water, and landed upright on the drain. Shimmering bands the color of clouds knifed through the pale blue water. Claire's shouts seemed to originate inside of my head, booming and mysteriously garbled.

I grabbed Harry by the neck and pressed my thumb against his Adam's apple. He pawed helplessly at my hands, kicked my shins like a child. Bubbles fled through his nostrils, and his eyes were wide with fear. I felt rich with rage and satisfaction: for once I had the upper hand. *Barry, Barry, Barry!* Claire shouted from above. Then Harry thrust his fists hard into my stomach, and I coughed out a lungful of air. That I couldn't drown Harry without drowning myself was an obvious fact I had failed to consider, and there we would be, identically dead, either loathing each other for eternity, or never seeing each other again. Claire's voice beckoned, calling only for me. I set Harry free and swam for the surface, feeling him rise in my wake.

Wildebeest

Wedging his feet onto the narrow ledges that were meant to serve as a ladder, Kenneth managed to climb up to the Jeep's elevated passenger seats without falling on his ass. His knees were arthritic, and he was thirty pounds overweight. He would have to get out of the Jeep in a couple of hours the same way he had gotten into it; that would be a trickier task, and he was already nervous about it.

"Careful there," the guide said. He was as brown as an acorn and wore pressed khaki pants. Alistair was his unlikely name. He hadn't said "careful" to Kenneth's wife, Gail, who had climbed up the Jeep like a monkey. Yoga was Gail's thing. If she were as flexible as she claimed to be, she would have been great in the sack, but it had been four years at least since they'd had anything resembling sex; they didn't even kiss anymore. Her excuse was that menopause had quashed her libido, but Kenneth knew other men his age whose wives still wanted to do it.

"Off we go, then," Alistair said in the clipped British accent that was as surprising to Kenneth as his name. He pulled away from the lodge and drove onto a rutted dirt road. Kenneth fastened his seat belt over his lap and hung his binoculars around his neck. Gail got her camera out of her daypack. When a rocky kopje came into view, she took a picture of it.

"Why on earth would you want a photo of that?" Kenneth said.

She shrugged. "It's a digital camera, I can erase it later." The camera was new and cost more money than they could have afforded six months ago, but six months ago they hadn't had the means to go to Africa, so she wouldn't have needed a fancy camera. Also new were her clothes, quick-drying slacks and blouses in earthy colors ordered from *TravelSmith*. And he and Gail had flown luxuriously in business class from Kennedy to Dar es Salaam. Previously, they rarely flew anywhere, and if they did, they went economy; they spent their summer vacations at Kenneth's mother's house in Westport on the Connecticut shore. Then, at the age of ninety-eight, his mother finally decided to die, and the wealth she had been hoarding since her own mother died had passed down, a windfall, to Kenneth.

Alistair stopped beneath the jigsaw shade of an umbrella tree and turned off the engine of the Jeep. "Giraffes," he said.

About fifty yards from the Jeep, a family of four giraffes ambled through a plain of tall grass. The stark morning light cast deep shadows; the horizon was pure white, aglow. One of the giraffes slowly bent its neck and tore a branch off a small leafy tree.

"Look at that," Kenneth said in astonishment. He'd never seen a giraffe before, not even in a zoo.

"Hush," Gail whispered, taking pictures nonstop. "There's a baby!"

The baby giraffe, barely taller than the grass, nuzzled its mother's belly. It was nursing, Kenneth supposed, or was trying to, anyway, for its mother walked away from it as if it didn't exist.

After a few minutes, Alistair started up the Jeep and they drove alongside a shallow stream. In the distance, a herd of elephants walked in an orderly line. Zebras grazed at the edge of the water. Kenneth felt his heart stutter as a gray bird the size of a small turkey flew across the hood of the Jeep.

"A kori bustard," Alistair said. "The largest bird in Tanzania."

"I hadn't thought about the birds here," Kenneth said. He hadn't thought much about the trip at all. Gail had planned the whole thing.

"Tanzania has over eleven hundred species of birds," Alistair said. He pointed at a colorful bird perched on the tip of a blade of grass that swayed slightly in the dry, dusty breeze. "That's a starling. Quite common."

Kenneth looked at the starling through his binoculars. Cobalt, teal, vermillion, orange: its colors were bold and iridescent, yet the bird was the modest size of a sparrow. The constant clicking of Gail's camera annoyed him.

"Why can't you just look?" he said.

"I am looking," she said.

"You're not. You're taking photographs. Can't you give it a rest for a minute?"

"No, I can't give it a rest," she said. "Don't be such a killjoy." *I deserve this trip*, she'd said when they were packing. Kenneth hadn't asked what she meant. But now he wondered why she thought she deserved this or anything else. It had been his mother who had died and, more important, who had lived for far too long. She'd been demanding and critical up to her very last breath—if anyone deserved a holiday, it was he.

The starling flew away. Alistair drove on until they came abreast of the elephants. Muddy brown from rolling in the stream, they swung their paintbrush tails and lazily flapped their ears.

"They're amazing," Kenneth said. Gail's camera clicked and clicked and clicked. He suppressed an urge to tear it from her hands and fling it out of the Jeep.

Alistair pointed out the largest elephant. "That one's a male. Male elephants are called bulls, the females are cows." The bull's tusks were long and streaked with red, as if it had gored some gigantic animal. Its hide was crusted with mud. "Usually bulls don't travel with the herd," he said. "He must be trying to mate." The bull stopped and turned and looked at them in what Kenneth thought was a disturbingly concentrated way.

"Why's he looking at us like that?" he asked Alistair.

"He's checking us out," Alistair said. "He can smell us, we're downwind. He'll move on in a minute."

"Don't you think we're too close to him?" Kenneth said.

"Oh, for God's sake, Kenneth," Gail said. "Don't be such a nervous Nelly."

Alistair smoothed his closely cropped hair and flicked away a tsetse fly. They were everywhere, unavoidable, immune to all repellents. Kenneth already had several angry bites on the flesh above his socks.

"I recognize this one," Alistair said. "The red marks on his tusks. Last week, I saw him not far from here. Elephants can be territorial when they're mating."

"In that case, he might not want us here, don't you think?" Kenneth said.

"It's rare for an elephant to threaten a human," Alistair said. "Really, it's humans who are the threat. Ivory poaching is a grave problem in the Serengeti."

"I would never wear ivory," Gail said.

Kenneth drew back and looked at her. There were plenty of things he'd heard her say she would "never" do, but wearing ivory wasn't among them. Not that she'd had the opportunity to. The only jewelry she'd ever been offered was a dinky sapphire engagement ring that he'd bought at a secondhand store in New London. Now he could afford the kind of ring he had wished he could buy back then. Maybe she thought she deserved that as well. Thirty years ago she had. How bright she'd been at twenty-three, not beautiful, but intelligent and eager. The first time he saw her, she'd been walking out of a sandwich shop in Westport with a straw bag on her shoulder and a brown paper bag in her hand. He'd dropped what he was doing and followed her all the way to the beach. It was as if they already knew each other; it was "fate," she'd declared. He supposed she'd call it "karma" today.

The elephant stomped the ground with one foot and beat the air with his vast gray ears.

"He's angry!" Kenneth said.

"Who are you, Dr. Doolittle?" Gail said.

Just then the animal raised his trunk and let out a deafening bellow that sounded exactly like the bellow of an elephant Kenneth had seen on a nature program.

"Hang on!" Alistair said. He put the Jeep in reverse and gunned the engine, driving backward at full speed without looking behind him. The elephant charged the Jeep, then stopped so abruptly that a golden fog of dust rose from his feet to his tusks. Alistair turned the Jeep around and sped back the way they came.

"I *told* you he was pissed," Kenneth said. He looked over at Gail. She was grasping the sides of her seat. "I told you so," he said again, because he couldn't tell if she'd heard him.

A formal lunch was served on the covered terrace of the lodge. Rectangular tables were draped with spotless white cloths, and a trio of uniformed waiters passed around platters of roast pork. Kenneth would have preferred a sandwich. He always ate a sandwich for lunch. When he asked for Diet Coke, he was served regular Coke instead. The view from the terrace was of a vibrant, velvety green plain several hundred yards below. In the far distance, a blue-gray storm approached, rain moving in misty sheets. It was a beautiful and strange tableau; Kenneth was mesmerized. He was startled from his reverie when the lodge manager stopped at their table.

"I heard you had quite an adventure!" she said. Pushing fifty, pale and plump, she wore bright red lipstick in a failed touch of glamour. Kenneth wondered if she had a boyfriend she was trying to impress, one of the waiters, or possibly a guide. Her accent was either South African or Australian. He couldn't distinguish between the two. "Unusual for an elephant to charge a Jeep. Now you've got a story to take home!"

"I thought I'd die of fright," Gail said.

"No worries! Alistair is our best guide," the manager said. "I'm sure you were never in any danger."

"I don't know about that," Gail said. She caught the eye of one of the waiters and indicated she wanted a second glass of wine by tapping her finger against the side of her glass. "My nerves are still jangling."

Genially, the manager drifted away to the next table, where a family of six—two adults and four boys—were making a lot of noise. The lodge was high-end, breathtakingly expensive, with sumptuous permanent tents that had private bathrooms, teak floors, and electricity.

"They must be rolling in it," Kenneth said, forgetting that he was rolling in it himself. Not being jealous of people who had money would take some getting used to. Gail was quiet, drinking her wine. She hadn't taken many photos after the elephant episode, though they'd encountered a pride of lions lazing under a tree, and a cheetah in pursuit of an impala.

"Kenneth, I think it's time we divorced, don't you?" she said. "We couldn't afford to before, but we can now."

Kenneth put down his fork. Making thoughtless pronouncements was a habit of hers that he usually indulged by not paying attention. "Oh, come on now," he said wearily. "What do you mean 'before'? We've never considered divorce."

"I have," she said. "I assumed you'd thought about it too. Of course, there wasn't any way we could have managed two households. I couldn't live very well on just what I make in real estate, and you've never made much at *Investments*."

"I'm the editor-in-chief!" Kenneth said. "I make plenty." Gail was right; he didn't really make much. He couldn't remember the last time he got a raise. The magazine had been losing advertisers for years. People got their business advice from the internet nowadays.

"Okay, you make plenty," Gail said impatiently. "But now that we have your mother's money, we can go our separate ways."

"*We* don't have anything," Kenneth said. "My mother left that money to me."

"I'm entitled to a portion," Gail said.

"I suppose you've looked into it."

"Yes."

"If you hate me so much, why did we take this trip?"

"I didn't say I hate you. I don't hate you at all; I just don't want to be married anymore. Come on, Kenneth. We haven't truly gotten along since Deborah went to college, and that was ten years ago."

"You married me because you thought I'd be rich," he said sullenly. At the time of their engagement, his mother had been diagnosed with breast cancer. Kenneth hadn't expected her to go into remission—he'd been told the cancer was aggressive—but she did go into remission and the cancer never came back. She'd ended up dying of a stroke. "What if I won't give you a divorce?"

"How absurd. I don't need your permission. Connecticut is a community property state, you'll be legally obligated to make a settlement." She put her napkin on the table by her plate. "I thought you'd agree we'd be better off separated. It was stupid of me to bring it up now; I should have waited until we got home. The wine went to my head." She scraped her chair back. "I'm going to take a nap, I'm beat."

She stepped off the terrace and turned down the dirt path to their tent. At night, the guests were escorted from the lodge to their tents by rifle-toting guards, and in the tent there was a portable air horn on the nightstand they were supposed to blow in case of emergency by pressing a red button on its handle. A sign on a table read "DON'T FORGET TO ZIP UP!" referring to the tent flaps, so animals wouldn't get inside. The idea of being surrounded by dangerous wildlife excited Kenneth, though he knew there wasn't any real threat. "You're much more interested in them than they are in you," Alistair had said.

He drank a second Coke and decided to take a nap too. Their tent wasn't far from the lodge, but the sun was very hot and he was sweating in a minute. It was even hotter inside the tent. Gail lay on her stomach on the bed, wearing only a pair of lacy underpants, perspiration glazing her body. From the back she looked like a young woman. From the front, she looked fifty-four, her face not unattractively lined. Kenneth lay down next to her, but got up again almost immediately.

"What are you doing?" she said groggily.

"I'm going to the pool," he said. "It's blazing in here."

"Don't forget to zip up," she said into the pillow, and was immediately asleep again.

The swimming pool was enclosed by a bamboo fence and surrounded by cushioned chaises. It was amorphous in shape, long enough for laps. But Kenneth wasn't interested in exercise; he hadn't been to a gym in years. No one else was there but a young woman sunbathing on a chaise. How could she stand the heat? he wondered. Her hair was very blonde.

"I suppose everyone is napping," he said.

"Probably so," she said. "I don't like to sleep in the day."

"Well, you're young, you have energy," he said. He waded into the pool up to his waist. The water was lukewarm and heavily chlorinated, not at all refreshing. He took a further step and was suddenly several feet underwater. He swam to the surface and took a ragged breath.

"I should have warned you," the woman said, laughing. "That's exactly what happened to me the first time I got in. The swimming pool is dug out of a crevice between the rocks." She pointed to the far end. "Watch out, there's a big one that sticks out over there."

"I wonder why they didn't just blast a hole," Kenneth said.

"That wouldn't have occurred to anyone," the woman said with a slight accent. "It's typically African to make do with what's at hand. We could learn a lot from them about acceptance."

Kenneth swam to the edge and looked up at her. Her white bikini was much too small. The low waist cut into her stomach and hips, creating a roll of tanned fat, and the triangles of fabric that were meant to cover much smaller breasts were slings that barely hid her nipples. Her face was a doll's in its round-eyed simplicity, rosy cheeks, and a plump pink mouth. An American woman would never let her fat hang out like that. He admired her lack of self-consciousness. "Sounds like you've been to Tanzania before," he said.

"I live in Kenya," she said. "Nairobi. I've come down to see the wildebeests crossing the Mara. I went to the river this morning. They've gathered, but they aren't ready to cross."

Kenneth frowned. "I have no idea what you're talking about."

"Really not? The Great Migration?" She sat up in her chaise. "The wildebeests swim across the Mara River this time of year, from Kenya to Tanzania."

Kenneth had seen many wildebeests that morning, with their

long, bearded faces and silvery coats, skinny legs and blocky bodies. They were ugly and uninteresting, he'd thought. He told the woman so.

"Oh, I know what you mean, they take people that way at first," she said. "They're not exciting like lions or leopards, the animals everyone wants to see. But they are beautiful in a different way. You have to get to know them. And the crossing is astonishing." She leaned forward, clasped her arms around her knees, and spoke with excited intensity. "They gather on the bank of the river and wait for days. Then suddenly one of them jumps in, and then they all follow. The river isn't wide, but it runs fast. Oh, the crossing is something to see. Wildebeest means 'wild beast' in Dutch. They are the bravest of the animals, I think."

"Is that what you are? Dutch?" Kenneth said.

"Yes, I was born in The Hague. My name is Jora, by the way."

"I'm Kenneth."

"You're American," she said. "Americans are always friendly."

Kenneth breaststroked to the opposite end of the pool, where there was a protruding boulder beneath the aquamarine cement. He perched on top of it and splashed his face and chest with water. Jora was about the age of his daughter Deborah, who lived in Los Angeles. Deborah was a "body worker," whatever that was, and worshipped a guru who was dead. She wasn't attractive; she looked like him. He loved Deborah, of course, but he thought now how nice it would be to have a daughter like this girl—or, better, a lover. But women her age were out of his reach. He felt old and deflated and not a little perverted. Then he remembered he was rich and felt happier. He slid down the boulder's curve until his head was submerged and his feet touched the bottom of the pool. He imagined Jora slipping into the water with him, her hair floating free around her face. He couldn't remember the last time he'd had a proper erection. But there it was, tenting his swim trunks as if he were a twenty-year-old.

"I'd like to see the crossing," he said when he surfaced.

"You need to be patient," Jora said. "It can take days before the wildebeests decide to jump in. They are working up their courage, I think."

"You go there day after day and just wait?"

She nodded. "It's kind of an obsession with me. I come down every year for it. But sometimes I don't get to see them cross before I have to leave. I'm only here for four days."

"Do you always stay at this lodge?" He tallied the cost of four days here and looked at her left ring finger. The diamond was the size and shape of a Scrabble tile, flashing in the sun. He wondered about her husband. Maybe he was a native Kenyan. For some reason he was titillated by that idea, doubtful though it was.

"I must go," she said. "Lovely to meet you." She gathered her sunblock and bottle of water and put them into a net bag. She slid her feet into a pair of silver sandals and put on a sleeveless dress over her bikini. "Maybe I'll see you at the Mara." She fluttered her fingers. "Bye bye."

He admired her sturdy legs as she walked away, golden and lightly muscled. For a few more minutes, he dallied in the tepid water, then got out and toweled off, refreshed by a dry breeze. He looked over the top of the fence at the bush that surrounded the lodge. In the distance, a giraffe stood in the shimmering heat, then disappeared—a mirage.

"Been swimming, have you?" the manager said. "Bloody hot today, yeah?" She was standing on the terrace, looking out at the same view that had earlier enthralled Kenneth. When she smiled at him, he could see that her lipstick had bled into the fine lines around her lips. The hems of his trunks were damp against his thighs, but the fabric around his waist and hips had nearly dried in the heat.

"I wonder if my wife and I could go to the Mara and see the wildebeests crossing," he said.

"The wildebeests? Sure, but the guides say they're not ready to cross just yet. You might be waiting a long time."

I've been waiting all my life, Kenneth thought. "I was told they could cross any time now," he said.

"Ah, you've been talking to Jora," she said. "Jora's mad for the wildebeests. It's up to you, but Alistair says there's a black rhino about. Now, they're a rare sight."

Torn, Kenneth considered. "I guess I could let Alistair decide."

"Excellent idea," the manager said. She clapped him surprisingly hard on the back before heading into the lodge.

Kenneth stood and watched her go, feeling vaguely dismissed. Considering the price he was paying for this safari, he thought he should be catered to. He heard the voices of the noisy family from lunch, and the clatter of cutlery and plates in the kitchen. He wanted a beer but didn't know where to find one, so he left the terrace and walked down the path. Jora came out of a nearby tent, wearing pants and a long-sleeved shirt. Her bright hair was pulled back from her face.

"Hello again," Kenneth said as they met on the path. "Are you on your way to the Mara?"

"I am indeed," she said.

"Do you mind if I tag along?" he said in a moment of inspiration.

"Tag along?"

"You know, go with you."

She shielded her eyes from the sun with her hand. "Don't you have your own guide?"

"Sure, but I thought it would be fun to go together. My wife's asleep. I'm on my own for the afternoon. No point in using two guides and two Jeeps when we could double up and go together." Jora crossed her arms over her breasts and squinted toward the lodge. He saw he'd made a mistake. Sweat sprung out on his forehead; he wiped it away with the back of his hand. He wished he'd gotten that beer. He'd be up at the lodge drinking it now, happy as a clam.

"I don't think that would be wise," Jora said evenly.

"I'm not hitting on you, for God's sake," Kenneth said. "I'm just being sociable. I don't care about the wildebeests, anyway. I'm going to see the black rhino."

Wordlessly, she walked on. He caught the scent of her perfume as she passed, as well as a deeper, womanly odor. *You stink*, he imagined telling her.

Gail was still asleep when he ducked into the tent and zipped the flaps behind him. She lay flat as a corpse with her arms and legs spread, snoring into the pillow. It was like her to take up the entire bed, he thought as he pulled off his swim trunks and shirt, resolving in that moment to give her as little money as possible if she pursued her idea of divorce. He went into the bathroom and looked at himself in the mirror above the sink. He had a double chin and was losing his hair, most of which was gray. His substantial belly was the color of skim milk, and his fading blue eyes—once brilliant, his best feature—were hooded beneath sagging lids. He thought of Jora. He was an old man to her. But he was only fifty-five! Gail tried to keep him on a low-fat diet and urged him to take daily walks, as if he had aged far beyond her. It occurred to him that the root of her demand for a divorce was another man—maybe she did want to have sex, only not with him. He stroked his penis until it was erect and went back into the bedroom.

He climbed onto the bed, straddled Gail's thighs, and slid down her underpants. Her eyelids fluttered as she woke. The moment he drove himself into her, she reared up and cried out. He held her down with one hand hard on her back as she struggled to turn over. She was his wife whether she wanted to be or not.

"Stop it!" she said. "Get off me! Goddamn it, get off!" She grabbed for the air horn on the nightstand, nearly within her reach, but it slipped away from her outstretched hand and fell with a clatter to the floor. She flailed her arms, bucked and twisted, kicked at him with her heels. Sweat dripped from his face to her shoulder blades and streamed into the valley between, but for all her yoga he was stronger. He would always be stronger than her.

Creamer's House

Creamer's house had been vacant for three years, ever since Creamer died. It was a big fieldstone rectangle with a kidney-shaped swimming pool that Creamer installed in the seventies, a brilliant blue blot surrounded by a flagstone patio that was hot as blazes in the summer. He'd been a widower for fifteen years before he died, and the inside of the house was a mess; when his children had it appraised, they were surprised to find that it was teeming with empires of mice. Still, the children sold it almost immediately to a family from Texas. But the Texas family ended up staying in Texas, and then it was on the market again.

A shared, unpaved driveway ran through William Prout's land, and the two men had often sat by Creamer's pool and shared a six-pack of beer. After the house went on the market a second time, William got the idea to buy it for his daughter Belinda, but the amount the Texans were asking was more than he wanted to pay. So the house sat eerily vacant, the surrounding grass growing tall and rough. Often, William would check the realtor's website to see if anything had changed. He had the money, he could have bought the house outright, but he wanted to get a deal. Eventually the Texans would reduce the price. His daughter Belinda and her husband Ron and their three children were crammed into a two-bedroom cottage, all they could afford on Ron's teacher's salary. William could use Creamer's land for his sheep, and his grandchildren would have their own bedrooms.

On a blowy afternoon in March, the sky a dire shade of purplish gray, William's ex-wife arrived with a pan of lasagna that she said was left over from a dinner party.

"What kind of lasagna?" he said, peeking under the foil.

"The delicious kind. Cup of tea?" she said, as if he were in her house. She lived across the river with her second husband, a man whom William had once considered a friend. Not a close friend, but someone he saw socially in the days when he had a social life. Edie had been the gregarious one, a member of every committee she could possibly be. Because of her cheerful persistence, she and William had managed to stay friendly.

She put the kettle on to boil. William closed his laptop. He'd been checking on his investments. For thirty years, he'd owned a profitable chain of hardware stores from New Haven all the way up to Providence, but he sold the lot of them seven years ago and retired to raise a few sheep.

"Creamer's house finally sold," Edie said.

"No, it didn't." He reopened his laptop, typed in the realtor's web address, and clicked on the thumbnail of Creamer's house. He turned the computer to face Edie.

"Well, Sally Warren told me she sold it this morning to a couple from New York. They paid the asking price, apparently. Sally was over the moon; she said she didn't think she would ever unload it."

"Sally?" William said. When he inquired about Creamer's house, he spoke to a man named Rick. "Who is Sally?"

Edie spoke slowly. "Sally is the realtor who sold Creamer's house."

"No, no, no," William said. "I'm going to buy Creamer's house."

"What are you talking about, William? Since when?"

"Since it went back on the market a couple of years ago."

"Why didn't you buy it?" Edie said.

"I plan to!"

Edie gave him a funny look. "William, the house has been sold, that's what I'm telling you. You can't buy it because someone else already did."

William stared at the computer screen. "It says here it's for sale."

Edie's purse was hanging by its strap on the back of her chair. She reached into it, felt around, pulled out her phone and punched in a number.

"Sally? Hi, it's Edie. Didn't you tell me you sold the Creamer place this morning? Right. Well, it's just that it looks like it's still for sale on your company's website. Yes, that's what I figured. Hold on a sec, would you?" She put her hand over the phone and said to William, "She says the website hasn't been updated yet, but the house is definitely off the market. Do you want to speak to her?" William shook his head.

The kettle shrieked. William went to the stove. He turned off the flame and reached into a cupboard for two mugs, took teabags from a drawer. "I planned to buy Creamer's house for Belinda and the kids, but I was waiting for the price to go down." He didn't know why it had never occurred to him that someone else would want it.

Edie sighed. "You're so goddamn cheap, William. It's absolutely your worst failing; it used to drive me crazy. You should have bought that house when Creamer died. Lord knows you have the money. It would have been terrific for you to have the grandkids next door, and poor Belinda and Ron, they hate living in that horrible little cottage. Shame on you, William, really. It serves you right for being such a scrooge."

William poured the boiling water into the mugs. He felt his chest tighten as he came to understand that he had truly lost Creamer's house. "Maybe…" He paused, his mind working. "Maybe I can buy Belinda that shingled farmhouse on Ferry Road instead. It's been on the market a year now, I bet I can get it for a song."

Edie stood up and put on her coat. "I can't listen to this, I'll go nuts."

He waited until she had gone out and shut the door before he picked up the mug he'd been about to give her and threw it across the room. Tea spun out of it like a Catherine wheel and splattered to the floor. He could see her through the window as she stepped off the porch, the wind tossing her careful hair. As the mug hit the wall, she turned away from the wind. For a moment he thought she would come back.

Trucks clattered down Creamer's driveway every morning at

seven, pick-ups, flatbeds, vans, coming and going and coming again, until they clattered away around five. The driveway was visible from William's kitchen window, as was Creamer's house; William had only to step out his door to hear the faint whine of electric saws and the *boom* of refuse being dumped. One morning he decided to walk down and see what was going on. The contents of Creamer's kitchen lay on Creamer's front lawn: a stainless-steel sink, a blackened range, a yellow refrigerator, an oven. A dusty worker carried a white porcelain toilet through Creamer's front door and tossed it into a dumpster with a crash. William followed the din of a jackhammer. The inside of the pool was being torn up into jagged pieces.

A man wearing khaki pants and a green padded vest came around the side of the house. He was barely a man, more of a large boy, with a head of thick sandy hair.

"Hello," he said. "May I help you?"

William pointed in the direction of his house and said over the noise, "I live up at the top of the drive..." The jackhammering stopped and he lowered his voice. "The former owner of this place was a friend of mine."

"I'm Harry Breen," the man said, and held out his hand. "I'm the contractor here. I didn't know the former owner. The property belongs to Lucas and Genevieve Zwerneger now. Is the noise bothering you? I'd be surprised if you can hear much. What are you, a quarter mile away?"

"An eighth," William said. "No, the noise doesn't bother me. Creamer was a terrific guy. Lived here for forty years. He put in that pool. It's a shame to see it dug up."

Harry looked at the ground and scratched his stubbled jaw. William knew he was being a nuisance, yet he thought Creamer's memory should be respected—that *he* should be respected.

"My daughter used to swim in that pool every summer," he said. "Maybe you know her? Belinda Prout?" But Belinda was almost forty now, he realized, years older than this guy.

"No, can't say I do. Thanks for coming by, Mr. Prout. Feel free to have a look around. Just be careful, and please don't go into the house."

William stayed for a minute until Harry was out of sight, then walked back home across the field, dew darkening the toes of his leather boots. The tree branches were budding red, and blades of new grass were sprouting, but the chilly air stung his face and bare hands. He stopped and looked back at Creamer's house, its windows empty but its stone indestructible; at least the shape of it couldn't be changed. "Zwerneger," he said, tasting the name. The other neighbors on his road had normal names: Smith, Davis, Holden.

When he got home, he phoned Edie.

"They're destroying Creamer's house," he said without saying hello.

"What?" Edie said. "They're knocking it down?"

"No, they're taking everything out of it. I've never seen such waste in my life."

"For goodness sake, that house is a wreck. I'd gut it too."

"Would you throw out the toilets?" William said. "A toilet is a toilet; they all work the same way."

Edie chuckled. "A toilet is definitely not a toilet, William. There are different models and colors."

He shrugged off his parka, hung it on a peg behind the door, and sat down at a long teak table Edie found years ago at a secondhand store in New York. She hadn't taken much with her when she left him, and he hadn't changed anything since. "I was just down there talking to the contractor, a kid named Breen."

"Oh, Harry Breen, he's the best," she said. "Everybody uses him."

"Is that so," William said irritably.

"William. Come on now. You can't really be surprised by this."

He looked out the window at Creamer's house and imagined the interior being stripped away until it was nothing but bare rooms and blank walls. When Creamer was alive, William could see his lighted windows at night and know where his friend was in the house. The kitchen, the den, the bedroom upstairs; by eleven the windows were dark. Like William, Creamer didn't go out very much, so when his lights failed to come on one January evening, William wondered where he was. At ten o'clock, he noticed that the windows were still dark, and he thought Creamer must have gone to Hartford to visit his son. But when he went to bed, he slept fitfully, waking often in the night, Creamer's withered face swimming around in his mind like a captured fish in an aquarium. At dawn, he rose and put on his clothes, and drove down the snowy driveway to Creamer's house with a strong sense of something gone wrong. He didn't need a key to let himself in. Like most people in their drowsy neighborhood, Creamer left his door unlocked. He found Creamer in the den, sitting in the plaid recliner he'd had for so long that the fabric on the footrest was threadbare. His legs were elevated, the TV remote was in his lap; there was a cup of coffee on the table by the chair. But the TV screen was dark, and the cup was full. Creamer was so long dead that he looked like an effigy, waxy-skinned and rigid as wood.

"I miss him," William said.

"I know you do," said Edie.

"Zwerneger," William said. "Jesus. What kind of name is that?"

"Life goes on, William," Edie said in a weary voice. "Try not to be tiresome about it."

William's ewes lambed in the middle of May, and he let the flock out to graze in the field between his and Creamer's place. Spring was his favorite time of year. The hostas and daylilies that Edie had planted around the house were pushing through the soil; the dogwoods were blooming pink and white, and the rhododendrons were getting ready to burst. The grass was so green it made him squint to look at it as he herded the bleating sheep. Once they ate one patch of grass down to the ground, he'd herd them to another area. He enjoyed their placid stupidity. They would follow him anywhere.

A long moving truck bumped down Creamer's driveway. William shaded his eyes with his hand. As the truck approached Creamer's house, a woman came out the front door. William could see her hair was dark; she wore a white blouse and jeans. He herded his sheep closer. The furniture that came out of the truck wasn't unusual: a long light-blue couch and two comfortable-looking red chairs, some rolled-up carpets, pieces of a four-poster bed. Genevieve Zwerneger came out of the house again as the movers unloaded more things. William didn't know why he'd expected the Zwernegers to be middle-aged, but that was what he imagined, even though Edie told him she'd heard they were young. Considering the price of Creamer's house, never mind the cost of the renovations, he'd assumed they were in their fifties—younger than *him* was what he'd thought Edie meant. Mrs. Zwerneger, Genevieve, looked to be no older than twenty-five. As if she felt his stare on her back, she turned in his direction.

"Hello!" she called and waved. Her voice was jubilant, her smile wide and white, the smile of a woman who had never been disliked. William ducked his head. "Hi there!" he heard her call again. He pretended not to hear. A black Mini Cooper convertible sped down the driveway, its wake a tsunami of dust. A tall man emerged from the car and bent to kiss the woman. Then he, too, turned and waved at William. William felt his face grow hot with embarrassment as he herded the sheep away.

When he got back to the house, Belinda and the kids were there. Belinda had inherited William's height and his pale blue eyes, but in the past few years she had lost her lankiness and gotten top-heavy and thick through the middle. She wore her dark blonde hair in a braid that trailed long down her back until it was pencil-thin at its end. Edie was forever frustrated by her refusal to "make an effort" with her appearance, but William thought Belinda looked fine as she was, or rather, he didn't notice how she looked.

"They wanted to play with the lambs," she said as a little girl and two older boys clung to William from his knees up to his waist.

"You should have seen how fast that Zwerneger character drove down Creamer's driveway!" William said. "He could have killed one of the kids."

"What do you mean, Dad? The kids are right here."

"But what if they'd been playing on the driveway?"

"Why would they do that?"

"They might have been!" William said. "My point is he just tore through here without a care. That driveway is unpaved, it's meant to be driven on slowly."

The children disentangled themselves from William and ran off to see the lambs. Belinda watched the boys climb the post-and-rail fence and the little girl wiggle through the lower rails. She shrugged. "Maybe they'll pave it."

"They can't pave it, it goes through my property, it's a right of way, you know that. They'd need my say so, and they're not going to get it."

"Well, okay!" Belinda said in an outraged voice meant to imitate her father. "I can't believe you're already picking a fight. Have you met them yet? What are they like?"

"I have no idea."

"I'm curious," Belinda said. "I'm going to go meet them." She got into her car and drove out to Creamer's driveway. William watched her park behind the moving truck and walk into Creamer's house. William went inside and phoned Edie, but Edie wasn't picking up. The only other person he wanted to talk to was Creamer. He made himself a cup of tea and watched the children through the living room window. The eldest boy held his little sister around the waist while she carefully petted a lamb's back; the younger boy walked around with his hands held out like Jesus among his flock. William imagined Zwerneger's Mini clipping his granddaughter, and he took a frightened breath. He stood up and paced the room, his heart beating a drum in his head. Belinda was gone a long time. When she came back, she smelled like flowers.

"They're incredibly nice," she said. "They showed me all over the house. I had no idea the place could be so elegant. They've done it over top to bottom, and they're planning to plant a vegetable garden." She sat down in the chair Creamer always took by the fireplace. "It was fun seeing what they've done. They must be zillionaires, but they seem very down to earth."

"Children," William said.

"No, I don't think so."

"I mean *they're* children."

"Hardly. They're around thirty, I guess. Maybe she's younger."

"It's ridiculous, a couple their age owning a property like that. And no kids, either. What are they going to do with all those bedrooms?"

Belinda sat back. "Probably they're planning on having kids. Or not, I don't know. What do you mean 'ridiculous'? Why shouldn't they own it?"

William looked into his tea, cold now; he'd hardly drunk any of it. He didn't have an answer because he didn't know what he meant. His anger rose like a fever. "Creamer's house was perfectly fine," he said. "It's just extravagance to redo it."

"Well, I wouldn't mind a little extravagance in *my* life," she said. "I'm not going to fault anyone else for having it."

William heard only humor in her voice. She'd never been a greedy girl, always grateful for what she had. That she'd turned out to be such a good daughter to him was pure luck. He'd been busy with the hardware stores when she was a child and hadn't paid much attention to her.

"I'm going to buy you a bigger house," he said.

She shook her head and laughed at him. "Oh, Dad, come on. Tell me another. You've been saying that for years."

There were a number of signs to choose from, but William saw the one he wanted right away. It was a bright orange square with a black silhouette of a running child on it and the words "SLOW CHILDREN AT PLAY." He bought it, brought it home, and nailed it to a stake, then stuck the stake into the dirt on the side of the driveway where Creamer's property ended and his began. He turned the sign toward Creamer's house. Then he went home and sat looking out the window until the Zwernegers came out around five-thirty. They got into their

Mini Cooper and sped out the driveway, kicking up a golden cloud that hovered in the air like a phantom.

William jumped up as they raced past and said, "What the hell?" He went outside and huffed down Creamer's driveway to where he'd put the sign. He pulled it up and replanted it closer to the road, almost in the road, where the Zwernegers couldn't fail to see it. Breathing heavily, he stood with his hands on his hips and gazed at Creamer's house. The Zwernegers had planted box bushes on either side of the door, and a fenced-in garden was halfway built in Creamer's part of the field. But all was still; the workers had gone home. He crossed the property line and approached the house, thinking to look in the windows, but it was a sunny evening and all he could see was his own craggy face in the glass. Then he did something he knew was wrong—knew, in fact, was illegal: he opened the front door and walked into Creamer's house as if he had a right.

Everything was different now. The only thing that appeared to be unchanged was the placement of the stairs. The Zwernegers had knocked down the wall between the den and the kitchen and switched everything around so that none of the appliances were where they used to be. Slate tiles replaced the old oak floor; the refrigerator was a silver monster. The room where Creamer died, where William found him, no longer existed. A trestle table and chairs stood in its general area, a flat screen TV on the wall. William recognized the flowery scent that Belinda brought back from her visit. A shallow terracotta bowl in the middle of the table was filled with dried rose petals and sprigs of lavender.

He walked back out to the front hall and into Creamer's living room. The formerly beige walls were bright ochre yellow, and a maroon and navy Persian carpet covered nearly the entire floor. The blue couch and the comfortable red chairs that William had seen coming out of the moving truck were positioned in a cozy group. A game of Monopoly was in play on a glass coffee table, and a book lay on the floor by a chair.

The brown stairway carpeting had been replaced by a blue-striped runner. His steps were silenced by its luxurious nap as he climbed to the second floor. The Zwernegers had taken Creamer's bedroom as their own, the first one at the top of the stairs, and repainted the walls a subtle seashell pink where in Creamer's day they'd been white. A spotless duvet lay on a four-poster bed like snow after a blizzard, and more lacy pillows than William could count were stacked against the headboard. He went to the window and looked out at Creamer's pool. The patio had been replaced by grass. The pool itself was no longer aquamarine, the only color he knew pools to be. Now it was the deep green of a woodland pond, narrowly bordered by blocks of rough stone. The evening light on the surface threw dappled reflections onto the walls, making everything around him shimmer and ripple, as if the room were underwater. It was pretty, he granted, both the room and the pool. He wondered what it all must have cost.

On top of a chest of drawers sat a gilded wooden box. He opened the box's lid and found a pirate's booty: rings, bracelets, necklaces; gold bangles and hoops; a thick silver chain; an enameled pin; a miniature ivory fan. He chose a pearl necklace and held it up to the light. The pearls were opalescent, cool, surprisingly weighty. He drew them through his fingers, silken against his rough skin, and gauged the length of the necklace by stretching it taut. Edie had a pearl necklace that her second husband gave her. She wore it all the time. The house and the pool and the fancy new kitchen; the smart little whizzing car, the Zwirnegers could buy whatever they wanted, it seemed, and the fact of it pissed him off. He poured the pearls from one hand to the other, feeling their heft once more, then tucked them into the breast pocket of his shirt and buttoned the pocket's flap.

Belinda was so surprised she staggered a little. William was delighted.

"Happy birthday!" he said. He held the pearl necklace like a bunting by its ends. "Put it on, why don't you?"

"My birthday isn't for two weeks," Belinda said. "Are those pearls *real?*"

"Of course they're real," William said. "They're just like your mom's."

"No, they're bigger than Mom's." She looked at him as if he'd told her he was terminally ill. "What are you doing, Dad?"

"I'm giving you a present," he said.

She still hadn't taken them from him. On the kitchen table was a pint box of fresh strawberries from the local farmer's market that she'd dropped off for him on her way home with the kids. The boys were doing cartwheels in the yard, while William's granddaughter, one finger in her mouth, watched with admiration.

"Don't go near Creamer's driveway, kids," he called through the open window. The eldest boy stood upright and gave him a puzzled look.

"Where did you get it?" Belinda said.

He hesitated. He hadn't thought she'd ask him that. It seemed like a rude question. "A store," he said.

"Well, take it back."

"What?"

"Return the necklace and get your money back. Thank you, but I don't want it."

"But why?" William said. He looked into his daughter's eyes and saw an emotion he couldn't precisely identify, something between anger and impatience. "Don't you think it's beautiful?"

"Of course it's beautiful," she said. "But in case you didn't notice, *I'm* not beautiful. I'd look like an idiot wearing pearls."

"That's not so," William said.

Belinda closed her eyes and pinched the bridge of her nose. She wore a baggy U Conn T-shirt and a pair of cutoff shorts, rubber flip-flops on her feet. She grabbed the front of the T-shirt and said, "What do you think, Dad, should I wear it with this? Or do you think it would go better with one of my other crappy shirts?"

"I don't know what you mean," he said.

"I mean where would I wear a pearl necklace? When I'm doing laundry? When I'm feeding the kids? Doing dishes? How about when I'm plunging a stopped-up toilet, which I do at least twice a week, or mopping the fucking kitchen floor? Do you understand what I'm saying, Dad? I don't live a pearl neck-lace life."

He'd never heard Belinda swear; she'd always been so gen-tle. He felt as if she might leap upon him and beat him with her fists. "You could wear them when you go out to lunch with your mom," he offered. He knew they ate at the Griswold Inn, which was fancy for around there. "Or on holidays…" he trailed off.

"Right. I'm really going to wear them in front of Mom." Her face changed to mock excitement. "Look, Mom, see what Dad gave me, a big fat pearl necklace! He never gave *you* one, did he?" She frowned at William. "Tell me a nice gift you ever gave Mom. Seriously, I want to know."

"Listen," he said. He held the necklace balled in one hand. *I'm upside down!* he heard one of the boys cry out. Now they were standing on their heads in the shade of a maple tree. He sat down so heavily the wooden chair squealed. "It's a present, that's all. What's wrong with that."

Belinda sat down across from him. "Look at me," she said. "No, Dad, *look*. Of all the gifts you could have given me, why a pearl necklace?"

"I don't know. I thought you'd like it."

Belinda laughed a single dry note. "Oh Jesus, Dad. There are so many things I would like, that I need, but a pearl necklace isn't one of them."

"Try it on, at least," William said. "I want to see it on you."

He handed the necklace to her and she brought it to her neck, lifting her arms to fasten it. The pearls pressed into her skin as she tried to pull the clasp ends together.

"It's too short," she said. "I can't get it around my neck. So even if I'd wanted it, you would have had to take it back." She stood up. "Gotta go. The strawberries are good. Don't wait to eat them or they'll rot." She gathered her children and they all climbed into her scuffed station wagon. "See you on Sunday," she called as she drove off, the kids waving at him from the back seat.

He dropped the pearl necklace on the table, where it gleamed against the unvarnished teak. He gazed out at Creamer's house, thinking he would have taken the grandkids to Creamer's pool on a hot afternoon like this, then later on he and Creamer might have shot the breeze for a while. The tears he'd suppressed when Creamer died finally filled his eyes.

The Zwernegers came out of the house and got into their convertible. William rushed out to his yard. The car hurtled past, trailing dust like exhaust.

"Damn you!" he yelled, shaking his fist in the air. Genevieve Zwerneger waved a cheerful hello as they turned off the driveway and sped away down the road.

No Diving Allowed

In Memory of Lee K. Abbott

Though the train was crowded enough that people were standing between cars, nobody immediately sat next to Gareth because he took up the better part of two seats. Half of his ass and his entire right thigh overshot his portion of the plastic bench; he used the remaining space beside him for his canvas overnight bag. But an hour into the trip, a teenager stopped in the aisle.

"Hey, man, do you mind? There's like nowhere to sit."

Gareth lifted his bag. "Be my guest."

The kid wedged in beside him and began to fiddle with his phone. Gareth would have liked to look at his phone, too, in case there was a text from his sister Marion, but he couldn't get at his pants pocket without shoving the kid off the seat. Feeling the kid's skinny leg pressed against his own, he was conscious of his soft enormity, though he had in fact lost thirty-two pounds since March and intended to lose a lot more.

He looked out the window. The summer-green world whizzed by as the train rocketed through the Connecticut suburbs. He watched for familiar landmarks—a pink Victorian mansion, a sloping street of tidy homes, a brick factory building renovated into swank residential lofts—until the train gradually slowed and the conductor called out his stop.

Marion was waiting on the platform wearing shorts and a sleeveless shirt, her slim legs and arms were brown and polished-looking, softly reflecting the baking sun.

"I'd like to take a picture of you right there," he said as he got off the train and hugged her. "Why do you look so fantastic?"

"How should I look?" she said. "Wretched?"

"Maybe a little," Gareth said.

"Oh, good riddance is what I say."

"I couldn't agree more."

"You never liked Barton," she said as they walked across the station lot to her car. Her short brown hair, the same color as Gareth's, took on a reddish tint in the sun.

"He made me feel like a second-class citizen," Gareth said.

"Me too. That's what happens when you marry up. That, and being cuckolded. Can wives be cuckolded, or is it only husbands?"

"Only husbands, I think. Is he still banging that woman?"

She shrugged. "Who knows. I don't care."

They drove down Main Street, past Darien Sports and the Tog Shop, Munn and Deal Interiors. To Gareth's mind, the town was such a conventional burg that simply driving through it made him feel depressed.

"Honestly, Marion, how do you stand it here?" he said, not for the first time. "If I were you, I'd move back to the city and get a real job now that you're single again." He didn't think her job at the local historical society counted as "real" because her salary was barely five figures. Before she married Barton, she'd made a good living as a paralegal.

"It's okay here," she said. "I like my job! Besides, technically I'm not single yet." She pulled into her driveway, turned off the ignition, and gazed up at the house. "I love this house. It's exactly the kind of house I fantasized about when I was a little girl. I dreamed I'd marry a rich guy and live in a big white clapboard house, and have a Labrador named Lucky." She turned and looked at Gareth. "And that's exactly what I ended up doing." As if to prove it, a large Lab named Lucky trotted around the corner of the house, her onyx coat gleaming, going dull, gleaming again as she moved from sun to shade to sun.

"You never told me that," said Gareth. In the many times he had visited her when she and Barton were married, she had never seemed entirely genuine. Madly cheerful and efficient, her voice shifting from clipped to demure, her gaze slid over him without connection: he never knew what she was thinking. Now that Barton was gone, his real sister had returned. He could even hear a far-off echo of Staten Island when she spoke. "What other fantasies having you been harboring, woman?"

She slapped his shoulder playfully and said, "They're too scandalous for your delicate ears. I baked a low-cal spice cake for your birthday. One slice is only a hundred calories, so it won't ruin your diet. I can't believe you're almost thirty."

"I'm almost twenty-nine."

"Well, twenty-nine is basically thirty." She was thirty-one.

Lucky popped up outside of Gareth's window and licked the glass with her huge pink tongue.

"Get *back,* you monster!" he shouted as he got out of the car. As a teenager, he had dreamed of being loved by a kind, handsome man—he dreamed of it to this day—but the rest of the story was pleasantly indistinct: he was in awe of Marion's specificity.

"So, is the reality as good as the fantasy?" he said as she bent to grab a bag of groceries from the back seat of the car. She stood and pushed her hair away from her forehead with the back of her free hand, balancing the grocery bag on her hip.

"Sorry," she said. "What did you ask?"

"Never mind," he said. It was a question too stupid to repeat.

"I'm dying," Marion said. "This heat is killing me. Let's go to the club and lie by the pool."

"It makes more sense to stay in the house with the air conditioning turned down," Gareth said. He and Marion used to leap through the sprinkler in the summer, and the only clubs they'd heard of back then were the Rotary and the Lions. He swatted away a dragonfly and ran his hand over a flowering bush of some kind, yellow buds and tiny knife-shaped leaves; a cloud of gnats flew out of it. Marion's garden was profuse and disorganized and smelled like a funeral. "I think you've overdone it with the lilies, sis."

She hooked her arm in his. "Come on. I don't want to be cooped up in the house all day. Wouldn't you love a swim?"

"I didn't bring a swimsuit," he said sullenly.

"That's okay, I have the one you left here last summer."

"I've lost thirty pounds; it won't fit anymore."

"Try it on, anyway. If it fits, you have to go."

"That's fine because it won't."

But it did fit. Not well, but enough because it had been too tight last summer. He looked at himself in the full-length mirror behind guest bathroom door. The swimsuit was neon green with a wavy pink stripe across the legs that made his thighs look as wide as tree trunks, but it had been the only one at Darien Sports he could squeeze into, and Marion had insisted he buy it.

"See? It fits. I knew it would," she said when he shyly stepped out of the bathroom. He wore the shirt he'd arrived in, a pale blue button-down with the sleeves rolled above his elbows. A purple bikini peeked through her lacy white cover-up. When they were little, they'd looked so alike that no one needed to be told they were siblings; Gareth hoped he'd be as handsome as she was pretty if he ever reached a normal weight.

The club pool was crowded with children and adults splashing and sunning themselves. Marion found two chaises together near the snack bar where the tempting odor of frying hamburgers vied with the summertime stench of chlorine. There was a constant stream of people on their way to order snacks and returning with milkshakes and bags of chips. Marion slathered herself with sunblock and stretched her arms luxuriantly over her head. Gareth straddled his chaise with his feet on the ground. The chaise's plastic straps cut into the backs of his thighs. Sweat trickled down his spine. He wouldn't have minded a milkshake. His empty stomach growled.

"Relax," Marion said, handing him the tube of sunblock. "Take off your shirt, for goodness sake."

Gareth unbuttoned his shirt but didn't take it off. A drooping roll of dimpled white fat concealed the top half of his trunks. Looking around, he realized there were hardly any men, just scads of children and their preternaturally attractive mothers, with a few anomalous plain ones thrown in. If Marion had given birth to a child, he thought, maybe Barton would have stuck around, but she hadn't. Gareth didn't want to ask why not and find out something tragic like she was barren.

"This place is a zoo," he said.

"Well, I won't be able to come here much longer. Barton has the membership. I only get to use it as long as I'm his wife."

"So get your own membership."

"Oh, right. Like they'd have me."

Gareth was surprised. "Why not? Of course they would. Who are 'they' anyway?"

"The membership board," she said. "They're all a bunch of snobs like Barton."

"You were good enough for Barton."

"Only for two years. Not really even that. Sometimes I think he married me because he needed someone he could feel superior to twenty-four hours a day." She shaded her eyes with her hand and looked at the pool. "Nobody talks to me anymore. All our friends are taking his side. Even women I thought were *my* friends, like Caroline and Harriet. It's as if I was the one who screwed around."

"Come back to the city," Gareth said.

"I want to stay in the house if I can."

"Some fantasies have to die, Marion. The house is just a house."

A sopping wet boy approached Gareth. "Hey, will you do a cannonball?" he said.

"A what?" Gareth said.

"A cannonball. You know, in the pool." A group of similar boys, eight or nine years old, stood a few yards behind him. Clearly, he'd been dared to talk to Gareth, and for that Gareth felt a wisp of sympathy. The boy was pretty: long black eyelashes, toffee-colored eyes; his wet, tanned skin was so smooth and unblemished that Gareth wanted to reach out and stroke it. He normally didn't give children much notice, but he could identify a gay boy a mile away. He wondered if the kid's friends sensed it. No, probably not yet. Gareth gave him a year or so before the other boys, and his own urges, made him feel like a freak.

"You want me to jump into the pool," he said. "You think I'll make a huge splash because I'm so big."

The boy rolled his eyes in the direction of his friends, as if to say it was their idea.

Marion sat up. "Where is your mother?" she said in a stern voice. "Does she know you're going around insulting adults?"

"Wait," Gareth said. "Okay, why not."

"Gareth, come on, no," Marion said.

"Clear the pool!" he shouted and took off his shirt. "Step aside," he said to the boy as the others scattered like jacks. He crossed the hot cement to the pool and leapt off its edge, pulling his knees to his stomach. Hitting the water painfully hard, the cold a shocking slap, he sank like a stone, bounced off the bottom, and hovered until he found his bearings. He contemplated the sky, wavy and pale, while floating as weightlessly as an astronaut in space. Freed from the heft of his body, he danced a silent ballet. When he ran out of breath, he shot up like an arrow through a school of silver bubbles. The surface was rocking as if a motorboat had sped through it.

"That was awesome!" said the pretty boy.

"Big splash, huh?" Gareth said.

The boy opened his arms wide. "Ginormous."

A whistle screamed. Gareth turned toward the sound. A young man wearing bright orange trunks was striding to the edge of the pool.

"No diving allowed!" the man shouted. Blond and muscular and deeply tanned, he was the lifeguard, Gareth realized.

"I didn't dive. I jumped," he said.

The man pointed at him. "This is a warning. Do it again and you're out of here."

Gareth saluted. "Understood." He swam to the steps and got out of the pool. His wet feet made tracks as he walked back to his chaise; water streamed from his trunks.

"You know what?" He sat down and picked up his towel. "That was a lot of fun. I haven't done a cannonball since I was a kid. I haven't been swimming in I don't know how long. That lifeguard is sexy, don't you think? This is a warning!" he said, imitating the lifeguard's barking voice.

Marion's face looked sunburned. She'd put on her sunglasses and hat. "I am incredibly embarrassed," she said. "Everyone was laughing."

Gareth turned and frowned at her. "So what, Marion? So fucking what? None of these people are talking to you anyway, why do you even care?"

"Why don't you care? You made a spectacle of yourself. Have some dignity, why don't you."

Gareth blinked and opened his mouth. Nothing came out for a moment. "Oh my God," he finally said. "You're ashamed of the way I look."

Marion slid down in her chaise, making herself small. "Of course I'm not ashamed. Don't be absurd. Why would I bring you to the pool if I was ashamed of you?"

"You baked me a low-calorie cake for my birthday," he said. "I was offended by that, to tell you the truth."

"Because you told me you're on a diet, Gareth! I was trying to be thoughtful!"

Gareth got up and walked away. He had no idea where he was going. He knew Marion was watching. He hoped she felt like a bitch.

"Hey, mister," a boy said to him as he passed. "Will you do it again?"

"Jason!" his mother said. "Leave the man alone."

"It would be my pleasure," Gareth said. This time next year he would be thin; he'd never make the same splash again. He took a few steps back to get a running start. "Out of my way!" he shouted as children fled in every direction. He ran to the pool and jumped as high as he could. The lifeguard's whistle shrieked even before he hit the water.

They drove home in silence, loathing each other. The minute they arrived, Marion stomped upstairs to her room and slammed the door behind her. Gareth went to the kitchen and found his birthday cake covered by a glass keeper. He took off the keeper and cut a big piece, settling himself on a stool beside a sleek marble counter before eating it without a napkin or fork.

The frosting was stiff and overly sweet with the tangy aftertaste of artificial sweetener; the cake itself was so dry it stuck in his throat and he had to suck water from the kitchen tap. Lucky sat thumping her tail on the floor, patiently waiting for a crumb.

"This is a seriously nasty cake," he said to himself. Knowing Marion, there was nothing good to eat in the house that didn't have to be cooked. She'd been the kind of kid who asked for fruit as a snack, while he'd craved ice cream and cookies. *Why can't you be like your sister?* was their mother's refrain as he grew chunky, then chubby, then fat. Mothers asked variations of the same question every minute of every day in every corner of the world, but his mother's widely fluctuating levels of outrage made it sound like a fresh idea every time.

"If it's nasty, why are you eating it?" Barton stood at the kitchen door, one hand in the pocket of his khakis, a manila envelope in the other. He wasn't a tall man, but he gave the impression of height because his head was disproportionately large. He leaned against the jamb and said, "What are you doing here, Gareth?"

Gareth put down the cake and brushed off his hands. "Marion invited me for the weekend. What are *you* doing here?"

Barton laughed shortly. "It's my house."

"And Marion's," Gareth said.

"No, actually, the deed is in my name," Barton said.

Gareth stared at him in disbelief. The jerk was going to take Marion's house. "I hear you've been fucking some babe at your office. Kind of a cliché, don't you think?"

"Where is Marion?" Barton said.

"Indisposed," Gareth said. "You better come back another time." In the meantime he planned to call a locksmith and have the locks on the doors replaced. Possession is nine-tenths of the law, he thought, though he wasn't entirely sure what that meant.

Barton laid the envelope on the counter. "See that she gets this, would you?"

"What is it?" said Gareth.

"Not that it's any of your business. Divorce papers. She needs to sign them."

Gareth leaned away from the envelope as if he expected it to explode. "But you haven't even agreed on a settlement."

Barton looked puzzled. "What settlement? We have a prenup. What's mine is mine, what's hers is hers. We go our own ways, end of subject. We've only been married two years, Gareth, how complicated could it be?"

"She never told me that," Gareth said. "She would have told me. I don't believe you."

"Maybe she doesn't tell you everything, have you considered that?" He gave Gareth a disgusted look. "I doubt you tell her everything about your life." He took a nylon leash out of his pocket. "Come on, girl," he said. Lucky got up and loped over to him. He clipped the leash to her collar.

"You're taking Lucky?" Gareth said as Barton walked the dog to the front door. "What kind of dick are you?"

"The kind that thinks you're a fat faggot," Barton said. "Tell Marion to call me."

After he left, Gareth went upstairs to Marion's room and knocked lightly on the door.

"I know you're mad at me, but we have to talk. Marion, come on." He opened the door and peeked inside. She wasn't there. He stepped in and looked around. It was a feminine room with pale green walls; glossy chintz in a pattern of stylized flowers covered the bed's headboard and an upholstered chair. A village of perfume bottles inhabited the top of a mahogany bureau— thoughtless gifts from Barton, he guessed, because as far as he knew, Marion didn't wear perfume. He examined the photographs on her bedside table. One was familiar because he had a copy: the two of them at a long-ago family party, his fat cheeks dwarfing her bright-eyed little face as they squished together for the camera. The pre-Barton days, he thought gloomily. The other picture was from her wedding. Because their parents were Catholic, she'd married Barton in church, but instead of a wedding dress, she wore a shell-pink shift and carried a single pink rose. Barton looked like he was on his way to work in a nothing-special gray suit.

He left the room and went back downstairs. Late afternoon

sun filled the panes of the living room's French doors, casting parallelograms of light onto the patterned carpet. He checked Barton's dim cave of a den, then went back to the kitchen. Her car was still in the driveway. He picked up his phone and called her. She answered on the first ring.

"Where the hell are you?" he said.

"Outside."

"Outside where?"

"The backyard."

He went to the kitchen door and opened it. She was sitting by the garden at the end of the yard.

"I saw Barton drive up. I knew he had the papers for me to sign, but I didn't want to do it with him standing over me. I sneaked out the front door and came back here while he was talking to you in the kitchen." She had on a white terry cloth bathrobe and her hair was tangled and wet, as if she'd rushed out of the shower. "It's true about the prenup. I could say I was naïve, but at my age that means stupid. He wanted me to sign it, and I felt I had to at the time."

"He called me a fat faggot," Gareth said. "I guess he's been waiting two years to say that. He took Lucky with him. I'm sorry."

"He bought Lucky. He bought this house. He bought me, if you think about it. I thought maybe he'd let me have the house because he knows I love it so much. But, no, of course he wouldn't. I'm the one who took care of the dog. God, he's such a jerk."

Gareth sat down beside her. "Did you love him? Do you?"

She shook her head. "I don't know. He wasn't even that nice to me when we were dating. But the sex, my God, it was incredible. I mean *multiple* orgasms. I'd never been with anyone so…" She frowned, as if trying to think of the right word. "Gosh, I really can't describe it."

"No need to!" Gareth said with a grimace. He didn't like to think of Marion having sex with anyone, never mind with Barton. He had never experienced anything close to incredible sex; it would be incredible if he had sex at all.

"I knew he wasn't in love with me," Marion said. "He's not really capable of love, I think. He wanted a wife and I was there. But plenty of couples aren't madly in love and still manage to get along. I thought I could make it work." She sighed. "I liked having nice clothes and a big house and being a member of a country club. Doesn't everybody want those things?"

"Some do." He took her hand and turned it over, stroked the lines on her palm with his forefinger.

"Well, maybe you think it's all bullshit, but it mattered to me." When he didn't reply she said, "Why did you do it? That second cannonball. You knew it would get us kicked out."

"Hubris," he said. When he surfaced there had been a ring of cheering kids around the pool; even some adults were clapping. The lifeguard continued to blow his whistle, but no one paid attention. For the first time in his life, his size was exceptional in an unambiguously positive way. "I'm the hero of the country club pool. They'll be talking about me for the rest of the summer."

"Well, it was an epic splash," she said. "I thought the lifeguard was going to burst a blood vessel." She had gathered their things and was walking out even before he ordered them to leave.

"It's not as if you're going to go back there," Gareth said.

Though she smiled, he felt her anguish. He regretted embarrassing her, yet he'd do it again. He watched an ant make its way through the grass, climbing over and around the blades. A cooing dove and a chirping cricket seemed to be speaking to each other. He would miss coming out here after all, the weekend respites from the city.

"I didn't mean to offend you with the cake," she said.

"I know. I'm not offended. I ate a piece. It tastes like shit."

"Oh, not truly like shit," she said. "You always exaggerate."

"*Always* is an exaggeration."

"That's a matter of opinion.'"

The scent of lilies grew heady; the sky turned from pink to blue. They sat in easy silence as the heat of the day subsided.

The Bottom of the Deep End

My mother's younger brother Patrick had been married twice, was single again, and was seeing a woman who wore pantyhose, even on the hottest days, and high heels to show off her long, lovely legs. "Look at those stems," Patrick would say, and Alicia would stretch out a toe. My mother said Patrick wanted to marry Alicia, but that he shouldn't because Alicia was common. Common or not, I didn't think she'd marry anybody, because at thirty-six she hadn't yet. Thirty-six seemed ancient to me. I was almost nineteen.

I had nothing to do because I hadn't made any plans. A gray lethargy had come over me in the winter and stubbornly outlasted spring, then all of a sudden I was home from college and summertime had begun. I didn't have a job and didn't want one, either; I hung out in my bedroom while my mother was at work, drawing and thinking and listening to music, until the sunlight abandoned my window, telling me the day was spent. I went downstairs when I wanted a snack, or to take a dip in the swimming pool. Often, Uncle Patrick would show up in the afternoon, and I would forget myself in the pleasure of lolling around in the water with him, exchanging observations. I didn't know what he did for a living. No one had ever told me, and I was self-absorbed enough not to wonder. He didn't ask what I'd been doing, or wanted to do, the way adults usually did, and I was grateful not to have to think up lies or make excuses for myself. There was always a gin and tonic sitting on the edge of the pool, mixed at my mother's bar. Slowly, he would sip it until the ice cubes rattled against the glass and our fingertips were prunes. There was a drought that summer, which refused to break. The grass between the pool and the house was tawny and stiff as bristles.

One afternoon he brought Alicia. They were already

swimming when I came out. I was disappointed not to have my uncle to myself. I dove into the deep end and swam the length of the pool.

"D'you have a boyfriend?" Alicia asked when I surfaced. Her own gin and tonic sweated on the coping next to Patrick's. Her reddish-blonde hair was piled on top of her head and she was wearing a full face of makeup. She swam with her head held high out of the water.

"I did," I said. "Not anymore."

She studied me. "You loved him." She said it with a certainty that was both comforting and odd.

"Yes," I said. Then I was embarrassed. "Not really. We only dated for a month."

Alicia looked at Uncle Patrick. "How long have we been dating?"

He smiled. "Dating? Is that what you call it?"

"Well, what do you call it?"

He took her in his arms and danced her through the water. "A love affair, my darling!"

"Oh, stop." She pretended to slap him and he fell back into the pool. When he surfaced his pale hair was flat on his forehead and water streamed down his face.

"You're a nice couple," I said. I had no such opinion—I had no opinion at all—but I wanted to insert myself.

"Oh no, we aren't," she said. "Let me tell you why. Your uncle here is of the upper classes, and I am—well, I'm *lowly*." She said this with humorous satisfaction. I looked at Uncle Patrick. He was smiling at Alicia. "Don't look at him," she scolded. "He's a fool. *I* know what's what." She breaststroked off to the center of the pool, a small wake lapping behind her. She turned around and said, "Oh, now, look at you, so woebegone. You're too pretty to look like that. I wish I had those big blue eyes. You could be a fashion model." I had been told I was pretty all my life, so the compliment had no effect. I wanted her to ask me if I was sad. I would have said I wasn't. Desperately, I needed to confess my unhappiness, but just as desperately I wanted to hide it.

"You know what you'd get a kick out of?" Uncle Patrick said. He wiggled his eyebrows the way he could, one seemingly independent of the other. "Going to the track."

"I've never been," I said.

"All the more reason," said Alicia.

The three of us turned at the sound of my mother's car crunching into the driveway. She got out and waved, then walked across the lawn to the pool. She'd lost a lot of weight when she and my father divorced, and she looked as straight as a wooden soldier in a silk blouse and a pair of slacks.

"Patrick, I hope you'll stay for dinner. Hello," she said to Alicia. Saying hello showed that she was a *lady*. Not calling Alicia by her name, and not inviting her to dinner, was her way of protesting Alicia's presence in her pool.

"We were just talking about the three of us going to the races tomorrow," Alicia said conversationally. I loved how unfazed she was by my mother.

My mother frowned at Uncle Patrick. "Take Sarah to Belmont?" When she shook her head, her peppery hair didn't move. "No, Patrick. Why would you want to drive all the way to Long Island in this heat?"

He winked at me when she glanced away.

"I saw that," she said. She pointed at me. "Absolutely not."

"Okay," I said. It didn't occur to me until later on that I was old enough to do as I pleased.

Uncle Patrick said he knew of a jockey whose horse bit off his thumb. "Then he spat it out on the ground like a plug of tobacco, and the jockey kept it in a jar of formaldehyde."

"Why didn't they sew it back on?" I said.

"This was long before things like sewing thumbs back on were possible. You weren't even a twinkle yet." He handed me a program with the page turned to the next race. "Take a look and see what horse catches your eye. Then I'll show you how to bet."

We were inside the clubhouse, high above the track, looking through a vast plate glass window. I could see the crowded grandstands below, where, according to Alicia, the riff-raff sat, and the hazy mirage of the dense neighborhood outside of the walls of the track. The clubhouse was air-conditioned and drinks were served there. It was full of people, but we were shown to a table right away.

On the track, there was a procession of sleek horses with jockeys, wearing garishly colorful shirts, perched on their backs.

"Each one is different," Alicia said about the shirts. "See the numbers on their backs?" She had let her brilliant hair down today, and it undulated in thick waves over her shoulders. She counted out some cash from her wallet and handed it to my uncle. "Stunning Heart to win, do you mind, Patrick?"

"Stunning Heart it is."

I chose a horse called Pythagoras because I liked its name. Uncle Patrick and I took an escalator to the betting level and stood in line to make our bets at a little window. There were dozens of windows, long lines at them all. The space was the size of a supermarket, and the floor was littered with torn-up tickets. Closed circuit televisions hung from the ceiling, broad-casting what was happening on the track. It was a weekday afternoon, but most of the bettors were middle-aged men. My uncle wore an open-necked blue shirt and a pair of white trousers, looking as fresh and crisp as a laundered sheet in that worn-out, dingy place.

"Win means first, place means second, and show means third," he said. "An exacta is when you bet on the first two winners; a trifecta is the first three."

We got to the window and I bet ten dollars on Pythagoras to win. I didn't expect to make any money. Uncle Patrick's bets were complicated, and he made them fast, dealing out bills like cards as he spoke. He bet on several horses at once.

"I like to bet a trifecta for the hell of it," he said. "It's the longest shot of them all, but if you win it, you win big."

"But don't you want to have a favorite horse?" I said.

"Nah. Horses are about as dependable as people. They'll disappoint you most of the time."

I thought, then, of the least dependable person I knew, the

too-handsome boy I'd dated for a month. When I told him I loved him, he said he loved me too, and then never spoke to me again. I was proud and disdainful of him to my friends, but when I saw him striding across campus, his dark curls tucked behind his ears, I felt a longing that I eventually came to understand was less for him than for the kind of mutual devotion that I imagined was the reason for living. Alicia and Uncle Patrick had it, I thought, in spite of the way Alicia talked. I wondered if I would ever stop feeling disappointed in myself for not having my love returned.

The horses were being led into the starting gate when we got back from making our bets. Then all of a sudden they were running. Alicia clapped and yelled, "They're off!" She sat on the edge of her seat, murmuring, "Come on, come on, come *on*!" Uncle Patrick looked intent, his eyes following the race.

My horse's number was fifteen; the jockey's shirt was purple and gold. It stayed back with the pack until the first curve, when slowly it moved up to third. I watched with fascination as it gained on the lead, edging through the others to the rail. It continued running in second place on the straightaway and as the horses rounded the final curve. At the very last minute it shot ahead and crossed the finish line in a dusty cloud. Uncle Patrick picked me up like a child and kissed me on both cheeks. People around us were talking and laughing. It was a sudden party.

"I won," I said. "Did I win?"

"Nine to one," Uncle Patrick said. "Do you know how much you'll get?"

"Ninety dollars. Eighty, less my ten."

"You're a winner!" Alicia said.

I burst into tears.

"Aw, honey," she said. "You're overexcited. Here, have some of this." She handed me her drink, an inch of dark liquid without ice. I took a sip and made a face. "Bourbon," she said. "Patrick, get her a rum and Coke." She waited for my uncle to go off to the bar before saying, "You're sensitive, aren't you? Like him."

I wiped my nose with a cocktail napkin. "Like who?"

She nodded her head toward the bar. "Patrick. He's sensitive too."

"I don't think I'm so sensitive."

"That's what he says too." She took my hand, turned it over, and pointed to a long line on my palm. "Your lifeline is chained," she said. "Your happiness is ecstasy, maybe too much so, but your sadness is no less than despair." She turned my hand toward the window to see it better. "You're creative. Well, people like you usually are." She patted my knee. "You'll feel better before the end of the summer."

"Is my uncle creative?"

"Yes, in his way. Now, don't you tell him I read your palm."

"Why?" I thought it was thrilling; I wished I could do it.

"It was how we met, you know. He came to me for a reading. That's right, I'm a professional palm reader and psychic. I bet you never would have guessed."

"What does his palm say?"

"That's none of your beeswax."

Uncle Patrick returned with my drink, and we planned our bets for the following race. I didn't say anything about Alicia reading my palm. I was glad she saw that sadness was in me. Being physically marked by the proof of it made me feel less ashamed. Patrick's pile of tickets lay on the table, all of them torn in half.

I touched them. "Didn't you win anything, Uncle Patrick?"

"There's always the next race," he said.

I was lucky and won two more races. Uncle Patrick said there were people who had a knack. When I asked to go to the track again, he refused and said, "Now you've got a taste for winning, and that's a dangerous thing." I didn't see how feeling like a winner could be bad. I was exhilarated for an entire day before I sank into gloom again. Uncle Patrick didn't come around for a week after that. When I saw him again, he looked pale.

"You've been going to the track without me, haven't you?" I accused. He smiled and sipped his gin and tonic, giving nothing away. Beneath the water, our bodies looked bloated and white.

My mother walked up from the house. It was Sunday, and she was wearing her church dress, a lavender sheath, but had come out of the house barefooted.

"What, no Alicia today?" she said to Uncle Patrick.

"No Alicia," he said.

I was surprised when she said nothing else except, "Dinner at seven if you want to stay," and walked back across the dry lawn.

I swam a lap and crawled up the steps. I sat at the top with my feet in the pool. It was a broiling day within a series of broiling days: I could hardly breathe through the humidity. Uncle Patrick leaned up against the coping, waist high in the water, dunking his head every now and then.

"Do you love Alicia?" I said.

"That's an awfully personal question," he said.

"Whatever."

"Sure, I love her."

"Are you going to marry her?" I said.

He shook his head no.

"Because she's common?"

He laughed at that. "Your mother's been talking to you. No, Alicia is about as common as a twenty-carat diamond. I'm not going to marry her because she won't have me."

I didn't know what he meant. "But she does have you."

"She doesn't want to have me forever."

"Why?"

"Why didn't your beau want you?" he said. "Your month-long love. What happened there?"

I was surprised he remembered that brief conversation; I hadn't thought he was listening. "He didn't want me because I loved him. No, because I wanted him to love me." I hugged my knees to my chest. "Recently, I realized that what I want more than anything in life is to be in love. Pathetic, huh?"

"No, not at all. That's what everyone wants."

He pushed away from the side and floated on his back. I wanted him to tell me something wise. He floated for so long that I felt compelled to ask, "Uncle Patrick, are you all right?"

"Not really," he said.

I was silent then. I didn't think he would tell me why, even if I wanted to know.

Finally, he dove down to the bottom of the deep end and hung there like a fish for what seemed like a long time. When he surfaced, he said, "How long was I under, do you think?"

"I don't know. A minute?"

He took off his big steel wristwatch and gave it to me. "Time me, okay?" Down he went again. I watched the secondhand tick.

"Forty-three seconds," I said when he came up.

"Now you try," he said. "Stay down as long as you can stand it. It's a game I played with my friends when I was a kid. Whoever could stay down longest won."

"I bet I can beat you," I said.

I gave him the watch and dove, blowing air slowly out of my nose. Uncle Patrick's legs looked sliced from his body; my hair was a swaying halo. I stayed down until I couldn't stand it anymore and beat his time by seven seconds.

I found Alicia's place a half a block west of the bus stop on a street of identical brick row houses. I rang the bell and waited a long time in the sweltering heat. I was about to turn around and go home when I finally heard a noise.

Her long robe looked like something out of a costume trunk, cobalt velvet with a braided gold sash. Her hair fell in damp tendrils from a topknot, and there were beads of moisture on her neck. I realized she'd been taking a bath.

"It's me. Sarah."

She smiled. "I can see it's you, Sarah. How in the world did you find me?"

"I'm so sorry. I should have called. I don't know why I didn't. I looked you up. I took a bus."

"A bus all the way downtown?" She seemed amused. "Well, good for you, I bet that was a first." She was right, I'd never taken a bus downtown before, and figuring out the route had been a puzzle. She showed me into a front room that was kaleidoscopic with paintings on nearly every inch of the walls: flowers and people and animals and fruit, landscapes, seascapes, portraits, foreign places. I felt a pulse start up behind my eyes as I looked around at them all.

"I love art," she said. "It's my passion. Or maybe a sickness!" She laughed. "If I see a painting I like, I have to have it." She sat down on a creamy white loveseat. There were matching armchairs on either side of it. She patted the sofa, and I sat down next to her. She took my hand and examined my palm. I watched her eyes for clues to what she saw. "Oh, you'll find love. Not soon, so keep that in mind. Don't go throwing your heart away to just anyone."

"Uncle Patrick loves you," I said. It was what I'd really come about. "But he says you won't marry him. Is it because you think he's upper class? The only person who cares about that sort of thing is my mother."

"Oh, that has nothing to do with it. Loving someone isn't always a reason to marry. Whether Patrick and I love each other or not isn't the point. Of course I love him, but I know we're not meant for each other. I'm a simple person; I like to look on the bright side if I can. Your uncle, he's not always a barrel of laughs. I'm not saying he doesn't know how to have a good time, but he knows how to give himself a bad time just as well." She unwound her topknot and let her hair down. I was conscious again of having interrupted her bath. "Never mind about Patrick. Let's talk about your life, honey. I can tell you're feeling better."

It was true. The darkness had lifted. I couldn't imagine why I had loved the boy; when I thought of him now I was astonished by his mediocrity. In a few weeks I would go back to college and take up my real life again. The summer seemed like a fitful dream, disappearing behind the light.

"You'll feel dark again," Alicia said. "Hopefully not for a long time. But you will suffer from it on and off all your life."

"Why?" I said.

She shrugged. "Feeling is equally a gift and a curse. Most people don't feel very much. Your senses cut you deep, and I'm sorry to say they always will."

She showed me out before I wanted to go. I decided to walk home instead of figuring out the buses, trudging through neighborhoods where women sat on narrow stoops, and teenagers lingered aimlessly at dim corner stores. These were blocks I'd never seen. Littered sidewalks and spindly trees. The tar on the streets had melted to taffy in the heat, bearing the impressions of tires. I walked for hours before I knew where I was and reached home in the early evening as the crickets took up their throb. I waded into the pool with my clothes on. Gazing up at a cloudy moon in a sky that was losing its light, I listened to my mother humming a tune in the house. She saw me and came out.

"You ever hear of a bathing suit?" she said. But she was smiling, and so was I.

A few days later, I found Uncle Patrick floating facedown a couple of inches below the surface of the pool, and for a moment I thought he was fooling around: I laughed and said his name. What bravery made me swim to him and take him by the hand? His skin felt like rubber with a hard layer beneath and was the grayish-white color of wax. I pulled him to the shallow end and anchored his body on the steps. I called my mother at work, and Alicia. I sat with him until the ambulance came and they made me let him go.

I told my mother and Alicia about the game Uncle Patrick and I played, timing ourselves with his watch. "We tried to stay underwater for as long as we could. I timed him; he timed me. He said he did it when he was a kid." We sat at the kitchen table, Alicia and my mother across from me. The room was unfairly cheerful, yellow paint and checkered linoleum. "I know it sounds silly, but we had fun. The more you do it the longer you can go. We'd push it until the last second. Uncle Patrick stayed under too long, that was how he drowned." I thought I made all the sense in the world, yet even as I insisted, a finger of doubt touched my mind.

"He was broke," my mother said. It was the first sentence she'd uttered. Shock and grief had turned her to stone. Uncle Patrick was her only relative. "He always needed money; he could never keep a job. I gave him whatever he asked for, he knew he could come to me."

"It didn't have anything to do with money," Alicia said. "You can't solve despair with a check."

"I know that," my mother said.

I felt like putting my hands over my ears. "It was an accident," I said through my teeth. The paramedics had given my mother his watch, and it lay on the tablecloth between us. I picked it up.

"He adored you, Sarah," Alicia said. "You should know that."

"You saw this was going to happen, didn't you?" I said. "You saw it in his palm."

She didn't deny it. Instead, she said almost angrily, "Do you think I could have saved him, Sarah? Don't you think if I could, I would have?"

Sullenly, I nodded. I couldn't imagine why someone so dearly loved could be sad enough to die. He wasn't loved enough, or in the right way; or he couldn't feel it, for some reason. *If only you'd married him*, I wanted to say to Alicia. But before I spoke, she took my hand and said, "I'd be a widow now if I had."

Minor Thefts

The swimming pool was empty because there was a crack in its side that needed to be patched, so Emma used it as a hideout when she wanted to get high. Bundled up in her purple down parka and a pair of silver Uggs, she would squat on the cement near a moldy accumulation of damp leaves, hoping no one would see the rising smoke or smell the skunky odor of the weed. But the pool was thirty yards from her house and half hidden behind a hedge; no one would think to look for her there—if they were looking, which they probably weren't. Her mother was busy getting divorced from her father, and her father had moved into an apartment. "My ex" was what Emma's mother called him to her friends on the phone with flat note of derision in her voice, though all of her friends had known him for years and the divorce wasn't actually final. Once in a while he would sneak back into the house when no one was home and take small but necessary things: a blender, a desk lamp, a marble cutting board for cheese. "Whatever. He can have it," her mother would say, but these minor thefts shocked Emma, the empty spaces where the things used to live. Why he took them was a question she didn't ask. She didn't ask either of them questions. No one would tell her the truth anyway, because even though she was fifteen, they treated her like a child.

One evening, her mother left the house in a cloud of perfume, her copper-colored hair done up in a chignon, her eyes heavily dosed with mascara. She returned at ten-thirty with a strange man.

"Say hello to Doctor Feinstein," she said in a compressed, mincing voice that Emma had never heard. Gleefully, she clapped her hands together. "Doctor Feinstein delivered you, Emma!"

"What do you mean 'delivered me'?" Emma said, thinking of the Domino's Pizza guy who sometimes sold her pot.

"He delivered you into the world," her mother said. "He was my doctor when I was pregnant with you!"

Emma looked at Feinstein. He was much older than her father. His hair swept over his shining pate in lonely single strands. *You've seen my mother's vagina*, she thought. She shivered in disgust.

"You were a loud one, came out wailing," Feinstein said.

"How can you possibly remember?" Emma said.

"It wasn't so very long ago," her mother said.

"But he must have delivered a zillion babies since then," Emma said.

"You were memorable," her mother said. "I was in labor for thirty-seven hours."

Emma also doubted that. Her mother loved to exaggerate. If she bought a bag of ten apples, she would call it a bushel; if it was warm outside, she'd say it was sweltering. Probably she'd been in labor for half a day.

Emma went up to her bedroom but didn't go to sleep. She listened to her mother's trilling laugh and Feinstein's heavy footsteps. First, they were in the kitchen—making drinks, she imagined—then they were in the living room, where their muffled voices rose through the floor. She crept to the stairway landing to hear what they were saying.

"It was such a pleasure running into you at the party!" Emma's mother said.

"Delightful," Feinstein replied. "You were always my favorite patient."

"Is that so?" Emma's mother said. "I missed you when you moved to Baltimore. I didn't like my new doctor nearly as much."

"I wasn't crazy about Baltimore," Feinstein said. "Too hot in the summer. I'm glad to be back in Connecticut." But he was bored by retirement, he said, and lonely since the death of his wife. She said she felt liberated by divorce. He said she was as beautiful as ever. She accused him of flirting with her. That was exactly what he was doing, he said. Then there was a silence.

"My goodness," Emma's mother said. "What a surprise."

"I hope I haven't offended you," Feinstein said. "I couldn't help myself."

Emma leaned over the balustrade as far as she could, but all she could see were Feinstein's brown leather loafers next to her mother's rose satin pumps. They were sitting close together on the couch; the silence must have meant they'd been kissing.

"Gross me out," she said under her breath. Now she had *that* image in her mind.

Often, the kid who lived in the house next door joined Emma in the pool. His name was Montague Wadsworth, which Emma would have teased him unmercifully about if she hadn't known him since they were little. He was seventeen and generous with his weed.

"My mother has a boyfriend," she told him the morning after Feinstein's visit. Monty nodded, as if this came as no surprise. His parents had been divorced for years.

"What's he like?" he said as he squatted next to Emma.

"Old," Emma said. She decided not to tell him Feinstein had delivered her. "They were kissing." She pretended to stick her finger down her throat.

"So what," Monty said. "You and I kiss all the time." He tucked his shoulder-length hair behind his ears and produced a joint from the back pocket of his jeans. He gave it to Emma.

"That's different, we're young," Emma said. She lit the joint and took a long toke. "My dad's coming to pick me up in a while. You think I should tell him?"

Monty shrugged. "If it'll get you something."

"What do you mean?" Emma said.

"You're new to the parental divorce game," Monty said. "If you tell your dad there is a potential replacement for him, he might buy you something you want so he'll look better than this guy."

"He does look better," Emma said.

"He doesn't know that."

"I get it," Emma said. She wasn't going to play the game. Her father had been fired from his position as the chief executive officer of a conglomerate that made everything from light bulbs to fertilizer, and Emma knew from eavesdropping on her mother's conversations with her friends that he was having trouble finding another job. Her mother's only concern was how her divorce settlement would be affected.

Monty stood and walked over to the crack that ran down the side of the pool to the drain. "I think it's getting wider," he said as he traced his finger over its jagged path. Emma took another toke from the joint.

"I'm cold. Let's go over to your place," she said, letting the smoke drift out of her mouth. Monty's room was above his garage, separate from the rest of his house; his mother and stepfather had let him move into it as a seventeenth birthday present. He and Emma had been having sex there nearly every weekend since then.

"I thought your dad was coming to get you."

"Oh, right." She looked at the time on her phone. "Can I keep this for later?" she said as she tamped out the joint on the cold cement.

"Knock yourself out," Monty said, and slid another joint from his pocket.

Scrambling up, she pulled herself over the edge of the pool, skirted the hedge, and walked casually to the house. Her father's BMW was in the driveway.

Her parents were standing in the kitchen looking like they wanted to fight. Her mother smiled automatically when Emma came through the door.

"Your father is here," she said.

"Where've you been, kitten?" her father said.

"Walking," Emma said. "Thinking." While her parents gave each other bewildered looks, Denise, the housekeeper, winked genially at Emma. Denise had only worked for the family for four months, after the housekeeper before her had retired. At twenty-six, she was close enough to Emma in age that Emma considered her an ally. Denise knew that Emma had sex with Monty above the garage, and also that she smoked pot in the pool. Emma didn't have to hide her stash on the nearly un-reachable shelf in her closet anymore the way she did when their former housekeeper cleaned her room. And Denise was pretty. Their former housekeeper had been a bony Estonian woman with a hairy black mole on her chin.

"Okay, off we go," her father said, and they walked out to his car. Emma threw balled-up paper bags and wrappers from the passenger seat into the back before she got in. She smoothed out a bag and looked at it.

"Arby's?" she said. "Seriously, Dad? Since when do you like fast food?"

"Since lately," her father said as he pressed the ignition but-ton. He backed the car out of the driveway and turned onto the road. "So, what's new with you, kitten?"

"Mom has a boyfriend," Emma said because she couldn't think of anything else. The weed was kicking in; the world went blurry when she moved her head. She turned on the element that heated her seat and dialed it up to high.

"She didn't waste any time," her father said evenly. "What's his name?"

"Feinstein," Emma said.

"Feinstein? Huh. She used to have a doctor named Feinstein. Years ago."

"That's him," Emma said.

"That's who," her father said.

"The guy. He was her doctor; Mom said he delivered me. Was she really in labor for thirty-seven hours?"

Her father gripped the steering wheel at ten and two. "Ridiculous," he said to himself.

"I know, right?" Emma said. "It probably won't last." She sat back and watched the familiar houses roll past, from enormous to merely big, until her father turned onto a busy four-lane road. It wasn't unusual for them not to talk while they were riding together in the car.

"No, she wasn't," he said.

"Who wasn't what?" Emma said.

"Your mother wasn't in labor for thirty-seven hours. It's pathological, the way she exaggerates."

"Oh, so that's why you're getting divorced," Emma said in a sarcastic voice. When they told her they were getting divorced, she hadn't needed to ask why. It was obvious they hated everything about each other; they fought like pit bulls in a cage.

Briefly, he took his eyes off the road. "I don't want to disparage your mother," he said.

"Oh, come *on*," Emma said. "You disparaged her every day when you were together. What? Did you think I was deaf? I heard you screaming at each other all the time, there's nothing I don't know."

"Shut up! Just shut up!" he said. Abruptly, he pulled the car into a Burlington Coat Factory parking lot and put his face in his hands. Emma thought he was going to cry. She felt around in the pocket of her parka and found the joint Monty had given her.

"Do you want some of this?" she said. "It might make you feel better."

"Where did you get that?"

"A guy," she said.

"You shouldn't be smoking pot. It's not good for your developing brain. How long have you been smoking it?"

Emma thought a moment. "I don't know. A while. I'm fifteen, Dad. What were you doing when you were fifteen?"

"I smoked some pot," he admitted. "And did many other more wholesome things."

"I do plenty of wholesome things," she said. She was on the volleyball team at school, for instance, though she wasn't sure if he knew it. She took a mini Bic lighter out of her pocket and lit the joint. She passed it to her father. He opened his window and threw it out.

"I would lose all custody of you if your mother ever found out."

Emma pressed her nose against the cold glass of the passenger side window, fogging it with her breath. "We only see each other once a week," she said.

"That'll change when I find a job and get a place where you can stay overnight."

"Okay," she said, though she didn't believe it. One afternoon a week was more time than she'd ever hung out alone with her father before her parents split up. He'd worked such long hours during the week that all he wanted to do on the weekends was rest. She didn't believe he would find a job, either, at least not very soon; many of her school friends' fathers were either unemployed or worried about keeping their jobs. A couple of kids had even been pulled out of Country Day and transferred to public school. She wondered if that would happen to her. She looked at her father out of the corner of her eye. He was staring straight ahead, hands on the wheel, as if the car was moving. Since they usually went to the movies on their day together, she asked, "What are we seeing today?"

He opened the car door, leaned out, and picked up the discarded joint. "Hand me that lighter, will you?" he said.

"What about your brain?"

"My brain stopped developing a long time ago." Holding the joint between his thumb and index finger, his other fingers raised, it looked as if he was signaling "okay" to someone outside the car. He leaned his head back, took a long toke, and blew the smoke in a thin stream against the car's ceiling, where it exploded into a cloud. He didn't offer Emma the joint, and for that she was glad. It was depressing watching her dad get high; he didn't look cool at all.

"My mom dated, like, twenty men before she met my stepfather," Monty said. "She went through them like potato chips."

Emma kicked off the bedclothes and looked down at her naked body, which had yet to develop beyond its initial pubescent sprout. Dim as a cave and overly warm, Monty's bedroom had the charm of a storage unit. There was his bed, his drum

set, and a chest of drawers; most of his clothes were on the
floor, emitting a faintly metallic stink.

"Did she sleep with any of them?" she said.

"A lot of them, yeah," Monty said. "I mean, I didn't like it,
but I could see why—she wasn't going to marry some dork
who was shitty in bed."

"Feinstein has been staying over a lot," Emma said. She disliked Feinstein more than she had anticipated. He talked to her
as familiarly as her parents did, offering up random advice as if
Emma cared what he thought. When she idly remarked that she
didn't know how to play golf, he insisted on teaching her next
summer; once, he suggested she brush her hair before the three
of them went out to dinner. Her mother's voice had returned to
its usual register, but she acted as if God had dropped Feinstein
from heaven, making sure his favorite obscure craft beer was in
the refrigerator and listening attentively to his every utterance.
Emma imagined such behavior took a lot of energy and hoped
her mother would get tired of it so Feinstein would move on.

She sat up and reached for her underpants at the end of
the bed. She liked Monty more than she liked anyone else, and
had sex with him because he wanted to, but she had yet to
understand why people thought sex was so great. He put his
dick in her and pumped for a minute, yelped like a kicked dog,
then pulled it out. She would have preferred to just fool around
with each other's bodies the way they used to when they were
younger.

"Are you going home?" Monty said.

"Yeah. Mom is cooking dinner."

"Where's Denise?" he said.

"Mom let her go. She said we can't afford a housekeeper
anymore." On Denise's last day, she and Emma had exchanged
phone numbers and promised to stay in touch. "Mom's selling
the house too," she said. "So, I guess I'll be moving soon."
What about us? she waited for Monty to say, like a lover in a
movie. When he didn't, her feelings were hurt—absurdly, she
knew; rarely did anything she saw in the movies seem like it

would happen in her life. "Hey, you want to come to dinner?" she said as she pulled her sweater over her head.

"No, thanks," he said. "Nicole Hale and I are going to a comedy club in the city."

"A comedy club?" Emma said, as if she'd never heard of such a thing. Nicole Hale wasn't beautiful but she was inexpressibly cool, and even if they didn't actually know her, everyone at Country Day knew who she was. Physically, she was the opposite of Emma, statuesque and dark, while Emma was ginger-haired, small, and lean. There was no reason Nicole Hale would know who she was because Monty never paid attention to Emma at school. Why didn't he? she wondered. Why hadn't she thought about it before? It was simply the way it had always been since the days when boys and girls publicly ignored each other even if privately they were friends.

She pretended the zipper of her jeans was stuck until she could compose herself. Her face was burning when she finally looked up.

"Sounds fun," she said. "Later, then."

Still in bed, Monty stretched his muscled arms above his head. "Yeah, later," he said through a yawn.

It was dark outside, and the temperature had dropped below freezing; her boots crunched through a fine layer of ice on the snow as she crossed from Monty's driveway to her own. Her eyes were swimming, but she didn't cry. She took her phone out of her coat pocket and tapped Denise's number. It rang several times before Denise picked up.

"What's up, Em?"

Emma wiped her running nose with the rough wool of her mitten. "Mom is still dating her gynecologist. They're sleeping together now."

"Fucking her *gynecologist*?" Denise said.

"I know, right?" Emma said. "How crazy is that?" Denise began to laugh, and then Emma was laughing too. She watched the clouds billow out of her mouth as she laughed and laughed. It *was* funny, she thought. Gross, but funny. "Do you think I should stop having sex with Monty?"

"Do you want to stop?" Denise said.

"It's just, he doesn't treat me like a girlfriend," Emma said.

"Then stop," Denise said. "Go out with another guy."

"What guy?" Emma said. "No one wants me."

"Oh, Emma, I don't think you realize how pretty you are. You'll be breaking hearts in a couple of years."

"Do you really think so?"

"I know so."

Marching in place so her feet wouldn't freeze, Emma said, "I don't even like having sex. He just does it and then acts like nothing happened."

"Been there," Denise said. Emma could hear the smile in her voice. "Listen, can we talk again tomorrow? I'm on my way out right now."

"Sure," Emma said.

"First thing tomorrow," Denise said. "Stay strong, Em. Don't let stupid people get you down."

"I won't," Emma said, and hung up.

The windows of her house were bright and warm. Her mother was stirring something in a pot on the stove when Emma walked in the kitchen door.

"What are you gawking at?" her mother said. She wore a pink gingham apron that looked new.

"You," Emma teased. "Cooking."

Her mother blotted her forehead with the back her wrist. "That's not fair," she said. "I've cooked for you and your father many times, and I make you breakfast every morning, in case you forgot. I used to cook dinner seven nights a week, you know, when your father and I were first married."

Emma sidled up to her and looked into the pot where gobs of meat and chunks of vegetables floated and bobbed in a bubbling greasy brown sauce. "When you were poor?" she said. Whenever her parents wanted her to know how lucky she was, they talked about the days when they were poor.

"Yes. Then," her mother said.

"Are we poor now?" Emma said.

"No, of course not," her mother said. "What's the matter? You seem tired. Are you tired? Where have you been?"

"Around," Emma said. She laid her head on her mother's shoulder and breathed in her sweet, musky odor.

"My baby girl," her mother said. "Why don't you take off your parka?"

Feinstein came in from the living room. "Emma! How are you?" he said as if he hadn't seen her in ages. In fact, she'd seen him at breakfast that morning. He'd read the *New York Times* while eating his eggs, a swipe of yoke on his chin.

"Pour me a glass of chardonnay?" her mother said. Feinstein got her a glass of wine.

"Can we tell Emma now?" he said in the wheedling, baby-talk voice they sometimes used with each other.

"But I thought we agreed to wait until dinner," her mother said.

"Tell me what?" Emma said. "Tell me now." She hated being surprised.

Her mother put down the spoon with which she'd been stirring the stew and took off her stiff new apron. "Doctor Feinstein, I mean David, and I—"

"Call me David, Emma," he said.

"David and I are engaged," her mother said. She smiled broadly at Feinstein, avoiding Emma's openmouthed stare. "Isn't it fun? Isn't it just terrific?"

"It's terrific," Feinstein said.

"You can't be engaged if you're married," Emma said.

"Well, we can't be married yet, of course, but we can plan to be," her mother said. "The divorce will be final soon, anyway. Your father and I have reached a settlement."

"You've dated for, what, a month?" Emma said.

"Five weeks precisely," said Feinstein. He chuckled. "Though we *met* sixteen years ago."

Don't let stupid people get you down, Emma thought. She would tell Denise she'd stayed strong. She zipped up her coat and walked back out the kitchen door into the frigid night. Her mother pulled the door open just as Emma shut it.

"Emma, come back here this instant!"

"I'm going to Dad's," Emma said without turning around. She walked down the snow-swept steps.

"I'm not driving you to your father's," her mother said.

"I'm not asking you to," Emma said.

"You can't leave!" her mother cried.

Emma walked away. She heard the door close. She knew her mother thought she'd be back in a minute. Looking up at the sky, she tried to choose one wish, out of all her wishes, to wish upon the evening star. She hadn't wished on a star since she was a child, before she learned that stars were merely planets reflecting the rays of the sun.

Her father's apartment building was less than a mile from her house, but she hadn't walked the distance before. She never walked anywhere—no one she knew did—so she felt conspicuous trudging beneath the streetlights along the suburban roads, cars whooshing by on the smooth tar, billowing white exhaust. The lights were on in the houses she passed: dim silhouettes of furniture and people, flickering television sets. She was perspiring beneath her parka, but her face was paralyzed by cold. She kept her hands in her pockets because she'd left her gloves on the kitchen table. She expected her mother to drive up any minute and demand she get into the car, but as car after car passed and didn't slow, she became determined not to turn back. Then, just as she was within sight of her father's building, a car did slow beside her. The passenger side window slid down.

"Hiya," said a man's voice from the darkness within. "You okay? Need a ride?"

"I'm fine," she said. "My dad lives right up there."

"Right where?" the voice said.

Emma pointed at the brick apartment building where her father lived. "The Greenwich Arms," she said.

"Come on, sweetie, I'll drop you off," the man said. "Get in, it's cold."

"No, I'm almost there," she said. The car stopped and the driver's side door creaked open. She didn't dare look at him.

"I'm Amos," he said. "What's your name?" None of your business, she wanted to say, but instinct told her to say a name, any name.

"Jennifer," she said. She stopped and turned as if she was going to get into the car, then pivoted and took off running. She heard only her own panting breath and the slap of her boots on the pavement. The cold air made her lungs ache. If she had to, she could identify the man. She'd seen him clearly in the half-second she'd turned. Small in stature, with a pale, narrow face and slicked-down mouse-colored hair, he'd worn a white shirt and a thin striped tie, a knee-length black coat, no scarf. Her father's building was a block away, then half a block; then she was there, pulling open the glass door to the wide, brightly lit lobby. The front desk attendant looked up. She whirled around and peered out the glass: the street was dark; the car was gone.

"Did you just see a car go by?" she said. "A silver sedan?"

"Nope," the attendant said. "Not that I was looking." He wasn't much older than Emma, a kid hired for a shift that nobody else wanted. He went back to the book he was reading. Emma walked over to the elevators and pressed the button between them. She leaned over, hands on her knees, and breathed several shuddering breaths. It was as if she'd dreamt the whole thing, the car and the man, his oily, cajoling voice. *Come on, sweetie.* Remembering it made her feel nauseated. She'd been so sure he was right behind her as she ran, snatching at the neck of her parka, but he'd gotten back into his car and driven off, and she'd been running away from nothing.

"There was a pervert out there," she said to the desk attendant, but he was engrossed in his book and didn't hear. The walls of the lobby were pale mustard yellow; the marble floor was beige. She thought it was the bleakest place she'd ever been. The elevator doors opened and she got in. As it went up, it made a skidding noise that sounded like it was scraping the walls.

On three, she got out and walked down a carpeted corridor that smelled strongly of roasting meat. 3A, 3B, 3C…different dinners cooking behind identical doors. When she knocked on 3F, her father answered right away. He wore a green terry cloth bathrobe that Emma's mother had given him a couple of Christmases before and held his wallet in his hand. On top of a small bookcase, just inside the door, there was a blue and white china bowl the size and shape of a pumpkin that had sat on the front hall table in Emma's house for as long as she could remember. Her father must have taken it recently, yesterday or the day before, because she hadn't noticed it missing yet, and she would have, she always did. It gave her a start, seeing it here, so familiar yet out of place.

"Emma!" he said. "I thought you were the food delivery. What are you doing here? Your face is red, are you all right?" He moved to block her view of the apartment, but she had already seen Denise sitting on the couch. With her blonde hair down around her shoulders and thick black makeup on her eyes, she was another version of the woman Emma knew, a recognizable stranger. She wore nothing but a plaid flannel shirt that Emma had seen her father wear on weekends.

"Hi, Emma," she said. Emma's father turned and frowned at her. "What? You want me to pretend I'm not here?"

"You're supposed to call me tomorrow," Emma said. It was the first thing that came to her mind before she understood that Denise was having sex with her father.

"Don't cry, Emma," Denise said. "Of course I'll call you."

"I'm not crying," Emma said. She had planned to tell her father about the man who tried to lure her into his car. Instead, she reached around him and grabbed the blue and white bowl. She would put it back where it belonged, and never let him take anything again.

Day Three

"I'm not *living* with my parents," I tell my friend Madalyn. "I'm *staying* with them. Moreover, they aren't even here. So, really, I'm house sitting. Doing them a favor while they cruise around Scandinavia."

"I know you are," Madalyn says. She's visiting from Connecticut. She comes back home every June for a few days to see her parents and her brother. Her husband, Paul, rarely comes with her, and I can't say I blame him; Madalyn's mother is a bitch from hell and her brother is missing a screw. She sips my secret recipe iced tea that I mix with a little Chardonnay—the Chardonnay being the secret, otherwise it's just Lipton.

"Also, Gus and I aren't getting a divorce," I say. "We're only taking a break. And I wasn't fired from the stationery shop; I quit because I was sick of it. People are saying I don't know what-all, but I'm telling you the real story."

Madalyn shakes her head and says, "I forget how small this town can be. Everyone gossips, but who cares what they say."

The thing is, I do care. I wish I didn't, but I do. I turn onto my stomach to get some sun on my back and undo the clasp of my bikini top so there won't be ghost marks on my skin from the straps. We're lying on chaises by the edge of the pool, dappled by the changing reflections of the afternoon light off the water. It's hot out, but neither of us suggests we go swimming. I don't want to get my hair wet, for one thing. Madalyn is wearing a floppy mauve hat and a pair of huge black plastic sunglasses that obscure the top half of her face. I'm almost positive she borrowed both items from her mother. She has zero style but she's smart as a whip.

"You're so lucky you got out of Richmond," I say.

"Luck had nothing to do with it," she says. "I wanted to get out, so I got out. You could have gotten out too. Still can, if you want. You're only thirty-one, Kate! You're capable of doing more than selling invitations." She speaks with a northern accent now, she says *lyfe* for *life* where I say *lahf*, I'm always startled by the difference at first. I sold custom invitations, I want to point out, which means knowing all about type fonts and different grades of paper, but I can see how some people might think the job is lame.

"I wonder what I should do next," I say into the plastic slats of my chaise. I wait for Madalyn to suggest something. Finish my college degree is always the first thing she says, but she just chews on a hangnail, she's not thinking about me. I wave my hand in front of her face. "Earth to Madalyn. Hello."

"I can't get pregnant," she says.

"What do you mean?" I say. "How do you know?"

"We've done four IUIs and three IVFs and none of them have taken."

I turn over and sit up, holding my bikini top against my chest. I didn't know she was trying to get pregnant. Her chin trembles a little like she might cry, and I know I should console her. But my feelings are hurt that she didn't tell me before.

"Paul checks out fine," she says. "And there's nothing wrong with me. The doctor doesn't understand why it's not happening. Jesus, even drug addicts can get pregnant." She sighs. "Maybe if I became addicted to heroin, I'd get knocked up right away."

I don't want children and can't imagine why people do, but Gus has a half-baked vision of himself as a dad. Never mind that I'd have to take care of the kid the way I take care of everything else. Gus's idea of "helping out" is spraying Roundup on the weeds in the yard. Not that I'm complaining, Gus suits me to a *T*, but the addition of a baby would be one human being too many. I know I can get pregnant because I did in December. I had an abortion pronto, Gus none the wiser.

"Gosh, Madalyn, I'm sorry." It's all I've got. I'm not going to tell her everything will be all right because I'm gathering from what she says that it probably won't. If Madalyn gave birth, it would be the first step toward the inevitable drifting apart that would end in the exchange of holiday cards and not a whole lot else. Give me a dime for every woman I wrongly thought would be my friend forever and I'd have a lot of dimes, but Madalyn and I have never lost sight of each other despite going our separate ways. She's an architect, and I'm a junior college drop out, currently unemployed. If anyone were going to have babies, you'd think it would be me for lack of anything better to do. "But you have a career," I say, as if this is urgent news.

"Yeah, so what?" she says.

"I don't know. You're important in the world."

She laughs. "Hardly. Do you know how many architects there are in this country?"

"Fewer than there are mothers, I bet." She frowns at me, or appears to; I can't see her eyebrows behind her sunglasses, but her mouth is severe, a thin line. "I'm just saying you're special, is all. You don't need to be anything more."

"I don't need to, I want to," she says. It seems to me that up until now Madalyn has gotten pretty much everything she wanted. She wanted to go to college up north, and she wanted to marry Paul from the moment she met him. She wanted to become a lawyer, which she did, and then she changed her mind and went back to school to become an architect. Last year, she designed and built her own home. I haven't been there, but I've seen pictures of it, and you would need quintuplets to fill it. I'm not saying I'm jealous, I'm saying her life has been charmed. It was only a matter of time before she hit a bump in the road, it happens to everyone, often more than once. For instance, when I was younger I planned on having a career in fashion, which obviously didn't work out, and for a while my goal was to be a personal shopper, but I had hardly any clients. I assumed I'd be with Gus until death do us part, but he says he needs time to "think about our relationship," so that assumption is temporarily on hold. My opinion is that our relationship is better than good precisely because we don't have to think about it. I couldn't stand the idea of being left alone in our house, just me in our king-size bed, so I came over here and he stayed at home.

I imagine he's missing me by now, not least because he doesn't know how to do anything for himself. I don't expect this break to last longer than a week. Today is only day three.

"You know what we should do? We should go out," I say.

"Out where?" Madalyn says sullenly.

"Drinking, dancing! Come on, it'll be fun. When was the last time you really let loose? Hey, remember the summer after senior year when we would drive to that bar out in the boonies?"

"Oh, that dump!" Madalyn says, but she's smiling, and I know I've got her.

For old time's sake we begin our evening with a drink at the dump in the boonies, which is even more rundown than it was twelve years ago, when it was the only bar we knew of that didn't card us. That Madalyn still likes rum and Coke makes me laugh. She says she shouldn't even be drinking at all because, you never know, by some miracle she might be pregnant. I order a martini and we sit at the bar along with a trio of construction guys and an old man who smells like a kennel. There are three women in the place not including us, and we attract our share of appraising glances.

"Here's to us," I say, raising my glass.

"And to better times," she says.

"Right," I say. "But let's not think about bad stuff tonight, okay? Let's just have fun."

A middle-aged construction guy is looking at us, giving me the creeps. He's bald on top and wearing a filthy coverall, and his face is as pocked as the moon. We're not here to pick up men, but then how would he know that? I give him a discouraging frown and shake my head in a silent "forget it," but he's not paying attention to me, his eyes are on Madalyn.

"Madalyn?" he says from across the bar. "Madalyn, is that you?" She looks up from her rum and Coke. He comes over, gazing at Madalyn like she's the eighth wonder of the world.

"Lance!" Madalyn says. "Oh my God!"

"I can't believe my eyes," he says. "Wow, you're all grown up and gorgeous. I bet you're famous or something now."

Madalyn laughs. "Not at all." She turns to me. "Lance taught me how to drive a stick shift right here in the parking lot."

"I did!" he says. "You were a natural."

They stare at each other, agog, saying what were the odds of meeting again and how have you been doing all these years, blah, blah, blah. I drink the last inch of my martini. I feel like I'm watching a movie about something that would never happen in real life.

"Madalyn, we need to go," I say after a few minutes. My stomach is growling and I'm certainly not going to touch the bowl of beer nuts on the bar.

She looks at me. "That's what you said the night Lance and I met! You wanted to go, and I wanted to stay. We had a fight about it in the bathroom, then you left, but Lance was a perfect gentleman and offered to drive me home."

"Well, do you want to stay *now*?" I say.

"I'll let you go," Lance says. "It was great seeing you again."

"I'm just amazed," Madalyn says.

I take her arm and literally pull her away. It's still light outside, and we are momentarily blinded as we leave the bar. My Corvette beeps when I unlock it.

"I would never abandon you in a bar," I say as we buckle up. I don't remember ever fighting with Madalyn, but she's not one to lie, and I wonder how many other fights I've forgotten in my life; I like to think I get along with everybody. The Corvette used to be Gus's until I took it for myself when he traded up to a convertible last month. The lingering smell of his aftershave catches the back of my throat.

"Well, you did abandon me," Madalyn says. "It doesn't matter. We were brats back then. You thought Lance was old and ugly."

"So he is," I say. "Not exactly our kind."

"You're such a snob," she says. "But he was nice to me when he could have taken advantage. I wish I could be that age again. Start over from scratch. That night, Lance said he'd like to meet me again in ten years, that he thought I'd be a formidable woman. I wonder what he's thinking about me now. I'm not formidable at all."

"You are too," I say. I put the car into gear and drive toward the highway that will take us back into town. There's a Mexican restaurant in the south end that serves killer margaritas, and a dance club nearby that I want to check out later on. "You're a big deal architect, that's pretty damned formidable."

"I'm not a big deal," she says. "I'm not even particularly successful. I should have stayed with the law, but I had a stupid idea that I was creative." She looks out the window at an undulating vista of greens. The Corvette rumbles over the road as I speed past lesser vehicles.

"Now stop that," I say. I have spent the better part of a decade admiring Madalyn; if she's not a success, I don't want to know it. "You're just depressed about not getting pregnant."

"I'm not just 'not getting pregnant,'" she says in a terse voice. "I've endured scores of hormone injections over the course of two years. I've miscarried three times, Kate. It's been a nightmare. At this point I just want to get pregnant so I won't have to try anymore."

I have a fucked-up urge to tell her about my abortion, maybe so she'll think I've suffered too. But I was in and out of the clinic in a matter of hours and haven't thought about it since. The last thing I want her to know is that I discarded the chance for a baby when she's so desperate to have one, yet it feels like the information is going to burst from my mouth. We ride in silence until we reach the wide stripe of the James River. Bulbous pink clouds appear to float on the water, moving surrealistically upriver.

"It's beautiful, isn't it?" Madalyn says. "Majestic."

"I don't even notice it anymore," I say. I remember crossing this bridge as a child and being thrilled and frightened by the rapid flow of the river. You would drown in a second if you fell into it, I'd thought, imagining disaster from the back seat of the car.

Gus always says I have a hollow leg, but he's one to talk. Let's just say that between the two of us we can put away a lot of liquor. Rosita Mexicana has the best margaritas in Richmond, but Gus doesn't like Mexican food, so I hardly ever get to come here. It's not a popular spot with anyone I know, but that's fine with me because I don't want to run into any of Gus's and my friends, Madalyn being the obvious exception. Though she was in our wedding party, and has known Gus for as long as I have, I've never heard her say she likes him, so after the waitress sets down my second drink, I get it into my head to say, "What do you think about Gus, Madalyn?"

"What do I think?" she says. "You mean about what he's doing now? I don't like it, of course. I think he's being self-indulgent. But he's always been crazy about you. I think it's a blip, an early mid-life crisis." She sucks up the last of her first drink through a straw. "You're right, this is delicious." She signals the waitress that she'd like another. "But I thought we weren't going to talk about bad stuff."

"But what do you think about *him*?" I say. "Do you like him?"

She looks surprised. "You've been married eight years!" she says with a laugh. "And you dated for four years before that. If I didn't like him, I think you'd know it by now."

"I didn't ask if you don't like him, I asked if you do like him," I say impatiently. I thought I knew the answer, but now I'm not sure.

I'm startled by how fast the waitress brings another drink. Madalyn immediately takes a long draw. "Of course I do," she says when she comes up for air. "I don't know why you're asking."

"Because I've never heard you say anything nice about him." The restaurant is crowded and we have to raise our voices to be heard. "Not once!"

Madalyn frowns. "Well, so what. I've never heard you say anything nice about Paul."

"I hardly know Paul," I say.

"You know Paul enough," she says. "He's been down here a few times. You visited us in Connecticut."

"I think Paul is the epitome of the snotty Yankee," I say. "I've never felt comfortable around him.

Madalyn's face flashes annoyance. "I'm not that crazy about Gus, either. We don't have to like each other's husbands." She's looking at something invisible in the space between us, and I think, uh-oh, she's had too much to drink. "The thing is," she goes on, "it's weird that we're still friends after all these years. We have nothing in common, really. Now that I think about it, we never did." She takes a bite of her chicken quesadilla. I nibble on a chip.

"Why did you say you like Gus if you don't?"

"Oh, because I'm used to him, you know? It's not that I actively dislike him or anything."

"I actively dislike Paul," I say. She nods as if this comes as no surprise. That she doesn't care what I think makes me mad. "Gus does a really funny imitation of Paul, he tilts his head back and talks through his nose."

"Huh," Madalyn says. She forks chicken and cheese into her mouth, chews and swallows before she speaks. "Paul says I talk like a hillbilly after I've been down here for a visit."

"God, how snotty is that," I say.

"You're the one who's snotty," Madalyn says. "'Not exactly our kind,'" she says in an ultra-drawling voice that's supposed to sound like mine. "I never understood why you act so hoity-toity, it's not as if you come from an old family. Your father owns a car dealership for heaven's sake." My mouth drops open and I feel my cheeks flush. My father owns several car dealerships and my family is much richer than Madalyn's. But her mother is a Daughter of the Confederacy and a Colonial Dame and that beats all around here. I wouldn't have credited Madalyn with giving that sort of thing any weight.

"You're right," I say. "We don't have anything in common." I'm sick to death of Madalyn with her graduate degrees and her northern accent, her urging me to go back to college and do better with my life. Maybe I don't want to do better; maybe I can't. I hail the waitress and indicate I want the check by pretending to write on my hand.

"Christ, Kate, I'm sorry," Madalyn says. "This is the stupidest conversation; I don't mean a word of what I'm saying. I just got into a bad mood. I don't know why. I'm taking my problems out on you." She taps her fingernail on the edge of her half-empty glass. "No more margaritas for me."

"I don't really dislike Paul all that much," I say because she's trying to be nice and I want to meet her halfway.

"Sometimes *I* do. I guess every woman feels that way about her husband now and then." I nod, though I don't agree. I have never disliked Gus. Sometimes we have spats, but they're over before you know it. I can't remember the last real disagreement we had, not counting the one three days ago, and I'm still not sure how that got started or what it was really about.

The waitress puts the check on the table and Madalyn takes out her wallet. "I'm getting this," she says as she counts out bills.

"Thanks." I don't care who pays the check; I just want to get out of here. It's later than I thought. I fish for my car keys in my purse. "I'll drop you home," I say.

"No, let's go dancing!" she says, taking a final draw on her drink.

I want to blow away the weirdness that hovers between us. You can say you didn't mean something, but the words don't disappear, they'll always be floating around like dust motes in the air.

The club we go to is so cool it doesn't have a marked entrance. There's a metal door in a featureless brick wall that a fat guy opens when you knock on it, then a long flight of stairs that takes you down to a large, dark room. The only light comes from neon bars on the walls that flash different colors in sync with the music. Cubic sectional couches surround the crowded dance floor, and there are high round tables where you can stand with your drink. Everything is black—walls, couches, tables, bar—so we have to wait for our eyes to adjust before we can figure out where to go. All of the couches are occupied, but there's an empty table. Madalyn stakes it out while I get us a couple of cosmos. I notice that almost everyone seems to be in their twenties. I used to be crazy about dancing, but I haven't done it in ages. I found out about this place from my next-door neighbor's twenty-two-year-old son ("It's the bomb," he'd said) but we were just shooting the breeze, I never thought I'd actually come here.

"We're too old for this place!" I yell over the music.

Madalyn shrugs and smiles. "Let's pretend we're not!" We sip our cosmos and people watch. It's too loud to talk much, but I'm content as the pounding music empties my mind. It's like being stoned without the pot, I think. I'm glad we came, too old or not.

"You know I love you," I yell at Madalyn. "No matter what. I'll never not love you, do you understand?" I'm drunk, of course, but I mean it. Madalyn is even drunker. She gazes at me with half-open eyes.

"God, I know, right?" she says. I nod. We understand each other. I lean across the table and kiss her on the mouth. It's not a sexual thing, just an expression of love. People are pouring in, and a couple of kids with multiple piercings ask to share our table.

"Let's dance!" I say to Madalyn. We weave our way through the crowd and step onto the packed dance floor.

I'm working up a sweat when yellow lights underneath the dance floor flash on, and everyone is brilliantly illuminated. There's a giant "rah" of appreciation and then we're all jumping up and down. Madalyn and I grab each other's hands and hold our arms over our heads. She's laughing and I'm laughing, the crowd around us is moving as one, then she abruptly stops laughing and her face turns to stone. She's looking at something behind me. She grasps me by the shoulders.

"We need to go," she says.

"But why?" I try to twist away.

"Because I feel faint." I always know when she's lying because she does this thing with her upper lip where she sucks it ever so slightly into her mouth. She'd make a horrible poker player.

"No, you don't," I say, and shake loose from her grip. I turn around and see Gus not three yards away, dancing with a girl. She has spiky pink hair and six hoops in one ear and is almost as tall as he is. One whole arm, from shoulder to wrist, is covered with a tattoo of twining roses. For a moment I think they're just dancing near each other, until Gus pulls her to him and buries his face in her neck. I tell myself he's someone who just looks like Gus, a guy with brown hair and boyish freckles, a little thick around the middle. But he's wearing a green-and-blue-striped dress shirt and a pair of cobalt blue chinos, both of which I bought for him the way I buy all his clothes. The girl dances away from him and dances back, shimmying against his chest. Gus's idea of dancing is shuffling from one foot to the other like a tone-deaf adolescent. Clearly she's not serious about him, but I can see he's into her. When he tries to kiss her, she dances just far enough away from him that he's left standing with pooched-out lips. I feel the way I did at the dump in the boonies, as if I'm watching a film. My eyes are throbbing and my chest empties out like water through a funnel. "Gus," I say in a wisp of a voice because I can hardly breathe. I start to go over to him, but Madalyn pulls me back.

"Come on. We're leaving," she says and leads me out of the place. We run up the stairs as if we're being pursued and bang out the door to the street.

"Was that Gus?" I say. I know it was, but I want Madalyn to contradict me.

"Shithead," she hisses. I sink to the curb. For the past three days, I've been imagining Gus sitting with his head in his hands, "thinking about our relationship," but I'm the one with my head in my hands, tears running down my cheeks. There was a rain shower while we were in the club. The air smells of hot pavement, and the curb is damp beneath me. I feel untethered by the idea of being single. Everyone I know is married. I realize I'd be six months pregnant now if I hadn't had the abortion, and Gus wouldn't think of leaving me.

"Who am I if I'm not Gus's wife?" I say.

"What do you mean?" Madalyn says. She sits down on the

curb next to me. "You're Kate, you're my friend, you're a human being."

"Imagine if Paul left you and you lost your job," I say. "How would you feel about yourself?" The truth is I was fired from my job at the stationery shop for telling a bride her choice of invitation was tacky. Usually people want my opinion, but not in that case, it turned out.

Madalyn claps her hand over her mouth, staggers to her feet, and vomits onto the street. Half-digested pieces of quesadilla float in a glistening guacamole soup, lit by the streetlamp above. "I'm seeing double," she says.

"We can't stay here," I say. I feel a little like vomiting myself.

We go to a little triangular park across the street, more of a traffic island planted with shrubbery. There's a bench where we sit down. Madalyn leans her head back and falls asleep, exhaling vomity breaths. Though I quit smoking years ago, I want a cigarette. The door to the club opens and a group of people come out, laughing and talking as they walk down the street and turn at the end of the block. Again, the door opens, and two women emerge, followed by a single guy. No one notices us. The street is empty of traffic. The air is cooler because of the rain; a light breeze dries my tears. I decide to wait here until Gus comes out. I don't know what I'll do after that.

Attractive Nuisance

A week after the Fourth of July, my dog Speedy nipped an eleven-year-old kid who wandered onto my property from the subdivision across the way. Speedy was a shepherd-husky mix and normally pretty docile, so I thought the kid must have been teasing him, asking for it somehow. The kid went home and cried to his parents, then his father came over and said he'd called the police. He was about a foot shorter than me and had a litigant's righteous air. But either he was bullshitting, or the police forgot to come, because that was the last I heard about it.

The subdivision used to be a sloping meadow, a hazy stretch of long, tawny grass speckled with wildflowers from May to September. A guy down the road owned it ever since I could remember, but then he moved to an assisted living facility and the land was sold. Not long after, skeletons of houses appeared, and within what seemed like no time there was a neighborhood of mini-mansions and smooth tar lanes, two curved stone entrance walls, and a big sign that read The Meadows at Glastonbury in fake-fancy gold letters. I planted a row of fast-growing spruces so I wouldn't have to look at the thing, and nailed up an orange No Trespassing sign on a tree by my driveway because I had a swimming pool behind my house and if somebody sneaked in and drowned in it I could have been held liable.

"He might still make trouble," my wife Sally said about the kid's father over breakfast a few days later.

"Trespassing is against the law," I said. "He shouldn't let his kid run around like that." I didn't have children and didn't care for them, so Speedy biting the subdivision kid bothered me not at all.

"For pity's sake," Sally said. "The boy crossed the road. How far did you go when you were a child? I was all over the place."

"There weren't any perverts back then," I said. Sally laughed at that.

"Remember razor blades in apples at Halloween?" she said. "I think that was one of those urban myths, but my parents wouldn't let me eat anything but the wrapped candies."

"My mother gave out popcorn balls," I said. "Kids loved them." I didn't really know if that was true. What was true was that I loved them, and my mother. I'd grown up in the house where Sally and I lived; I bought my brother's half when Mom passed.

"Maybe I'll make a batch of my oatmeal lace cookies and take it over." She cocked her head toward the subdivision as if she meant to bring cookies to every house.

I took a third piece of toast and coated it with strawberry jam. "You don't know where they live."

"They live on Buttercup Lane. In the *Gone with the Wind* house. It's got a row of two-story pillars out front, couldn't be uglier if it tried."

It was so typical of Sally to know such a thing that I didn't even bother to ask how. "If you bring them cookies, they'll think we're sorry, which implies guilt on our part."

"Oh, now, shut your mouth," she said good-naturedly. I was her second husband, and I usually did as she asked because I wanted to be her last.

I met Sally at an Al Anon meeting two years ago. She was there because her second husband was a drunk, and I was there because of my older brother, who used to get pie-eyed and berate me over the phone about my supposedly superior attitude. Though I was a corporate attorney and he was unemployed at the time, the only reason I felt superior at all was that I didn't get drunk every night. I was loving him a little bit less every day, and his accusations had been wearing me out, so I decided to go to Al Anon one evening at the suggestion of a friend at work. The thing about Al Anon is you stand up and pour your heart out and then it's crickets. I hadn't known that before I'd gone, and it gave me the creeps: I felt like I was talking to a school for the deaf. I had already decided I wouldn't go back when Sally came up to me afterward.

"I have a sister like your brother," she said. "Only she isn't a drunk, she's just a bitch."

She didn't look like the kind of woman who'd call anyone a bitch, never mind her own sister. Her pale braids were wrapped around her head and she wore a puffed-sleeve shirt that was printed with little flowers.

"What do you do about your sister?" I said.

"I haven't talked to her in years," she said. "Life is too short to be involved with toxic people."

"Well, your husband sounds pretty toxic," I said. She had described an incident in which she locked herself in the bathroom while he broke everything breakable in the bedroom.

She stared at me as if my hair was on fire. "You're right! But I never think of him like that."

"How do you think of him?" I said.

"I think of him as he used to be. He was the nicest guy you ever met."

I nodded. "Not anymore, I guess."

She asked me if I wanted to go for a drink, so we went to a wine bar around the corner. Then we drove back to my place and sat by the neon light of the pool and ate coffee ice cream from the carton. The way she ran her pointed tongue over her lips was the sexiest thing I'd ever seen, but eating ice cream and talking about ourselves was all we did that night. The next week, I went back to Al Anon just to see her, and we did the same things again, but this time the night felt like a sauna, and she tore off her sundress and dove into my pool.

"Turn around so I can get out," she said.

"The pool is lit up, Sally. I've already seen it all."

"In that case." She got out of the pool. Water streamed from her shoulders and breasts; her hair wept down her back to her waist. Her bikini underpants were glued to her body, showing a dusky triangle between her thighs.

"You can't be naked and expect me not to be turned on," I said.

She smiled. "I don't expect that."

There was a stack of towels in the pool house. I got one and wrapped it around her. "What about your husband?" I said.

She tucked the end of the towel between her breasts and said, "Oh, he's passed out by now."

On summer Fridays, I left work at one. Everyone in my office did. I'd eat some leftovers and watch a game on ESPN, then take a late afternoon swim. Sally was usually painting in her studio upstairs and wouldn't knock off until supper. When I walked in the door at about 1:15 and heard her voice from the kitchen, I thought she was talking on the phone.

"Of course it's terrible," she said. "Nobody should be treated like that. But there are bullies at every school."

I went into the kitchen. "What's going on?"

At the table was a dark-headed little boy who was eating an oatmeal lace cookie. His left arm stopped where his wrist should have been; instead of a hand, there was a ruddy, thumb-shaped appendage. It was a shocking sight, and not a little repugnant. I tried to feel sorry for him but was just thankful he wasn't mine.

"This is Macon," Sally said. "The boy Speedy bit." Macon looked at me out of the corner of his eye. Speedy was sweeping the floor with his tail, waiting for a handout. Sally talked to me over the kid's head. "Macon's parents work all day while a girl from the neighborhood watches him. But when I went over to The Meadows with a plate of cookies, I found her smoking a cigarette on the front steps and talking on her phone. Macon was inside playing video games all alone on a beautiful day like today. What's your babysitter's name, Macon?"

"Kylie," Macon said. "She's boring. All she does is smoke and talk to her boyfriend, and the only sandwich she makes is peanut butter. I'm not a baby. I don't need a sitter."

"Macon's family just moved here from Chicago," Sally said. "Isn't that right, Macon?"

"Well," I said, because I didn't know what to say. Neither Sally nor I had ever referred to the subdivision as The Meadows and hearing her say it unsettled me. The kid took another cookie.

He was wearing a yellow polo shirt and red shorts and a pair of brand-new Nike sneakers. "I've got this thing I need your help with," I said to Sally, and she followed me out into the hall.

"Poor boy," she said before I could speak. "I doubt he's had an easy time of it with that arm. I knew a girl in grade school who only had three fingers on both hands. I wasn't very nice to her, I'm ashamed to say." She sighed. "You know what? That babysitter is a piece of work. She ought to be fired. You'd think she was going to a funeral, wearing black from head to toe."

"It's against the law to take a child from his home, Sally. What if his parents came home unexpectedly? You could be charged with kidnapping."

"Don't be ridiculous," Sally said. "I already called his mother. She sounded relieved, actually."

"That a stranger has her child?"

"She knows who I am; it turns out we've met before."

"Where on earth?"

"At Mary Yarrow's baby shower. I thought her name sounded familiar, and I was right. We both gave Mary a set of onesies."

I knew Mary and her husband Chester; they had an obscene number of children. "How does Mary know her?"

"Book club," Sally said shortly. "I know what you're thinking, and we're not going to disturb you. He brought some toys with him and we're going to sit outside."

"What about your work?" Sally was a magazine illustrator and juggled deadlines like duckpins.

"Things are pretty quiet today," she said. "I could use a break anyway."

They disappeared from the kitchen and I stood over the sink with a piece of steak and a beer, gazing out the window as I gnawed the meat from the bone. The spruces hadn't grown quite high enough to hide the subdivision. I wondered why Macon's parents had chosen to live there instead of in a regular neighborhood: the houses looked grand, but they were cheaply constructed, with featureless cement walls behind their fancy facades. The sun beat down on the browning grass; heat waves rose from the tar. The trees were no taller than I was. I'd never seen any kids over there, but I hadn't been looking for them either. When I was a kid, I had my brother to play with and plenty of friends at school. My mother stayed home to take care of us and was always a benevolent presence, purveyor of Band-Aids and snacks.

I washed my hands and went into the den. From there I could see the backyard. Sally lay on the grass looking up at the sky, the full skirt of her pink cotton dress spread as wide as its pleats would allow. She was in the habit of lying on the grass and studying the sky, as if the answers to life's mysteries would drift down like snow. Macon drove a plastic truck around her, using his good hand. My first thought was that Sally was going to get grass stains on her dress, which was one I particularly liked; my second thought was that Speedy should have been inside with me instead of sitting out there watching Macon's truck as if it were a live rabbit. I opened the window and whistled for him. He looked up at me and broke into a run.

"That's a good boy," I said when I let him in. We settled down in front of the TV to watch a Red Sox game. After a while, he started whining like he needed to pee, so I let him out and watched him mark a shrub. Then he went over to Macon and sat next to him while the kid played with Sally's phone. Macon was kneeling on the ground, a rapt expression on his face, tapping the keys with his good thumb as well as his bad one, which apparently worked just fine. What on earth could have happened in the womb to produce a stunted arm with a thumb on the end of it? I grimaced, thinking about it. His skin was the color of skim milk, and he looked like he needed more to eat than peanut butter and lace cookies.

"Speedy," I called. "Speedy, come *here*!" It wasn't until Sally sat up and shooed him away that he came running back to me.

The next week, on Thursday, I came home early because my allergies were making me miserable. Macon was in the backyard, throwing a ball to Speedy. I watched as he made a few feeble throws before I took off my suit coat and joined them.

"How come you're not afraid of Speedy?" I asked. "After he bit you and all."

"He didn't mean to," Macon said. "We were playing. My arm got in the way of his mouth."

Which arm? I wanted to ask out of a kind of sick curiosity. "Then why'd you send your dad over here?"

"I didn't. He saw where Speedy bit me and made me tell him what happened. I *said* we were playing. I don't know why he got mad." He looked up at me with almond-shaped brown eyes. They were spaced so far apart I thought of those pictures of aliens with eyes on the sides of their heads. He was going to have a hell of a time finding a girlfriend, I thought.

"Let me show you how to throw that ball the way he likes it." I took the ball and threw it hard against a tree. Speedy sprang up when it bounced off the trunk and caught it cleanly in his mouth.

"Wow," Macon said.

"Keep your wrist straight," I said. "Don't let it flop around or people will say you throw like a girl. Where's Sally?"

"Inside."

"I figured that much myself." I went inside and called for her. She came down from her studio upstairs. "Is he here every day?" I said as she stood looking down on me from the second-floor landing. She was wearing her paint-splattered work smock and a pair of frayed jean shorts, her hair in two pigtails tied with green yarn.

"Macon?" she said. "More often than not."

"I don't think that's smart," I said. "Especially as you're not watching him."

"I can see him from my window upstairs."

I shook my head. "Not good enough. You can't see the pool from there, and what if he falls in? He could drown in an instant."

She came down the steps and kissed me lightly on my lips. She was wearing the lilac perfume I had given her for Christmas and smelled like springtime and paint. "Believe me, he's not interested in the pool. He doesn't know how to swim." She looked at her watch. "What brings you home at this hour?"

"So if he fell into the pool he'd *definitely* drown? No, honey, we can't have him here."

She reached into the pocket of her smock for a stick of Juicy Fruit. Chewing gum was her only vice. "All right, fine, I'll stay with him," she said as she peeled the foil from the gum. "I can work in the mornings before he comes over."

"Why are you so determined to have him here?" I said.

She folded her arms over her chest. "Why are you so determined not to?"

"I just told you why."

She turned and stalked into the kitchen. "Macon?" she yelled out the back door. "It's time for you to go home."

"Come on, Sally, don't be like that. I didn't mean he had to go home right this minute."

Macon came in. She put her palm on the back of his neck, a gesture that startled me in its intimacy. "Lord, you're hot, Macon. It's about ninety degrees out there."

"I'm okay," he said. He looked up at me without raising his head. I felt like the big bad wolf.

I was almost choking from post-nasal drip and my eyes felt like they'd been pelted with sand. I left the kitchen and went upstairs to the bathroom for the allergy medication I'd forgotten to take that morning. When I came down again, I heard Sally's voice.

"Some people are just angry for no reason, and even though they act like they're mad at you, it doesn't really have anything to do with you, it's all about their own problems."

I went to my den and dug into some work I needed to finish that day. Sally's footsteps creaked above me as she walked around our bedroom. I rolled my chair away from my desk.

"Sally?" I called.

"What?"

"Can I talk to you a minute?"

She came down and stood in the doorway, tapping the jamb

with her bare toes. "I was just about to take a shower," she said.

"Why were you saying all that about me?"

She frowned. "All what?"

"What you told Macon. That I'm angry for no reason."

Her face cleared. "I wasn't talking about you, for goodness sake, why would you think that? I was talking about Macon's father. You saw how he was when he came over here. He's one of those men who're always jonesing for an argument, and Macon is afraid of him. Isn't that awful, to be afraid of your father?"

"Plenty of people are," I said. My father had been a quiet man, the opposite of my garrulous mother. He read to my brother and me in a whispery voice full of drama and checked under the bed for monsters when he tucked us in at night.

"I think it's terrible. He sits around with that awful girl all day long and then his father comes home and yells at him."

"Okay, you don't have to play a violin," I said. "He can come over in the afternoons, but keep a sharp eye on him, Sally, I mean it."

She rolled her eyes at me. "I *mean* it," she mocked. "You've gotten so bossy. When did that happen?" She pivoted away and sprinted up the stairs. A minute later I heard the gurgle and moan of water running through the pipes.

"You've got two problems, as I see it," my brother Kip said. I could just imagine him sitting back in his chair and putting his feet up on his desk. My "problems" were nothing compared to his, but he'd been sober for over a year, and we could talk on the phone now like normal human beings. "The first problem is you're jealous."

"Jealous!" I said. "Of what?"

"Sally loves the kid, obviously."

"Sally doesn't love the kid, she feels sorry for him."

"Whatever," Kip said. "You've always been possessive of Sally."

"What do you mean? Is that really what you think?"

"I think you're the lucky one."

"Gee thanks," I said, though I knew it was true.

"Plus you hate kids," he said.

"I don't hate kids, I just don't want any. I'm almost forty, they'd tire me out."

"If you say so." He paused to take a drag of a cigarette. He'd taken up smoking when he stopped drinking, giving him a necessary distraction while lopping years off his life. "The second problem is you are incredibly paranoid about people falling into the pool and drowning. It's weird. Why don't you put a fence around it? I can't believe your insurance agent hasn't already told you to do that."

"He did. I ignored him." I had landscaped the pool area with a flagstone patio and clouds of pink and white rose bushes that flowered all summer if I made the effort to deadhead them. A maple tree had once shaded the deep end and dropped its wing-shaped green pods in the spring; I'd cut the tree down when I bought the house, and now the water reflected the sun all day long as if it were a tropical sea. I swam before work from June to September and drank a cocktail on the patio on fine evenings. I couldn't imagine a fence—or rather, I could. "It would be hideous," I said.

"Oh, and worrying every minute about a lawsuit is better," Kip said. "It's an *attractive nuisance*, am I right?"

"That's the legal term for it, yes." Kip had done a year and a half of law school and knew a smattering of jargon that he enjoyed airing out now and then like old pillowcases from a trunk. He'd been selling timeshares on Cape Cod ever since he dried out.

"It seems like a pain in the ass," he said.

"Who's jealous now?" I said.

I didn't think I was possessive of Sally. Even if I'd tried to be, she wouldn't have tolerated it. She had dozens of friends from every stage of her life and made new ones all the time. I wasn't surprised that she wanted to help Macon because she was kind to everyone that way, the chief confidante of her women friends, the first responder to every crisis. But her friends weren't in the habit of coming over every day. I wondered if she did love the boy. Though she said she didn't want children, maybe she'd changed her mind. She would be thirty-seven in a little more than a month; technically it wasn't too late. Having someone else's kid hanging around was far preferable to having my own. I considered the truth of that before picking up the phone.

"Do you think I'm possessive of you?" I asked her.

"Sure," she said distractedly.

"I am?"

"Listen, baby, I'm busy," she said. "I'm on deadline, and Macon is here. He's playing with my colored pencils. He's pretty good at drawing."

"It's a beautiful day," I said. "Why isn't he outside?"

"Because you told me to watch him," she said in a severe voice. "Now, for goodness sake, let me go."

"Never," I said, which made her chuckle. She hung up without saying goodbye.

I chose a wooden post and rail with a welded wire screen that I was assured would be practically invisible. Of all the choices— picket, chain link, electric wire, to name a few—it was the most natural looking and would weather to a mellow gray. I could imagine growing climbing vines on it, clematis or what have you. The guy said he couldn't install it until September.

"What's the point then?" I said. But if you offer enough money, you can make almost anything happen, and a few days later a Fences Plus flatbed truck heaped with wood pulled into the driveway at six o'clock, and five brawny guys arrived a few minutes later in a handful of busted-up vehicles. I hadn't told Sally because I wanted to surprise her, and by the time she got up most of the posts had been sunk.

"What is that?" she said.

"I'm putting in a fence."

She stared out the window at all the activity. "But you always said a fence would be ugly."

"It's relatively attractive as they go," I said. "You won't have to worry about Macon falling into the pool anymore."

She looked at me. "I never worried about that. You worried about that."

"Well, the pool is an attractive nuisance, and now we'll be compliant with the law."

"Attractive nuisance!" She laughed. "*You're* an attractive nuisance." She turned and went to get dressed.

I walked out and watched them bang in the posts. Some rails had started to go up. A guy was unfurling a bale of wire. When I came back from the office at half past one, the fence was complete, and the Fences Plus flatbed was gone. Macon was sitting on top of a fresh wooden rail, looking at the pool. It never occurred to me that he could climb it. Speedy was watching him avidly, at the ready for I didn't know what.

"Get down from there," I said. "That fence is meant to keep you out."

"Why?" he said as he climbed down.

"Because you don't know how to swim," I said meanly. I could have put it another way.

"I do a little bit," he said. "I can dog paddle."

"You can dog paddle with that arm?" It was the first time I'd mentioned his arm to him and I felt my face go rubbery with embarrassment.

"You'd be surprised how much I can do with this arm," he said, squinting up at me. "I'm going to camp next summer. My mom says I'll learn to swim there."

"You don't know how to swim at your age and you're going to camp? You ought to know how before you go, or the other kids will make fun of you."

He looked down at his feet and rubbed his nose with his fist. "So what," he said to the ground.

That moment, I saw Macon's life unspool like a reel of a disturbing film. He was the kid who was pushed around in school hallways, his books slapped out of his arms. Ignored on the playground, shut out of games, the butt of jokes he didn't understand, he'd go to camp and be teased and tormented there and it would all be the same to him. He couldn't throw, and he couldn't swim, and his father was a dick. All of that and a gimpy arm added up to a kind of childhood misery that I could only imagine.

"My dog likes you better than me," I said. It was the only compensation I could think of.

"We're pals," he said. "But he likes you best."

"Listen, do you have a pair of swim trunks?" He nodded. "Go and get them. I'll wait for you."

I walked to the house and called out for Sally, shedding my suit coat as I climbed the stairs. She came to the bedroom door.

"You were right. The fence looks fine," she said. "We can grow some honeysuckle or something over it."

"That's what I thought." I found my trunks in a dresser drawer.

"Going swimming?"

"Yup."

"Okay, I'll be in my studio. Have you seen Macon?"

"I saw him when I came in."

Outside, I tested the gate in the fence. It had a metal hasp if I chose to lock it. I walked in and looked around. The fence really wasn't so bad. I sat down on the chaise where I had courted Sally with a carton of coffee ice cream. The pool's surface was glassy, and the sky the kind of bright, sunless white you saw on humid days. Macon ran around from the front of the house wearing a pair of striped swim trunks. He clambered over the fence.

"There's a gate right there," I said. Maybe he heard me, maybe not, but I never did see him use it.

Dulaney Girls

Loretta checked into the Hampton Inn in Hartford rather than a bed and breakfast near Dulaney Hall because she hated the smothering coziness of B and Bs, their doilied surfaces and cabbage rose upholstery, bed linens redolent of the musk of past guests. None of her former classmates who still lived in the area had invited her to stay with them—Barbara Grant, for instance, or Helen Bromley, girls she'd once considered friends. But that was understandable; she hadn't seen them since 1987.

"Oh my gawd!" Helen said when she saw Loretta at the alumnae luncheon. They were seated next to each other. The same old yellow cafeteria had been decked out with cloth-covered tables, plates with golden school crests, and crystal goblets that cast rainbows in unexpected places, such as Helen's powdered cheek. Helen hugged Loretta and gave her the once over. "My, aren't you stylish."

Loretta looked down at her clothing, a long black skirt, black suede boots, and an emerald green blouse she'd bought in Japan that wrapped her slim torso in layers of silk. She touched her necklace, a strand of pre-Colombian stone beads that one of her ex-husbands had given her. Nobody else in the room was wearing black. Royal blue appeared to be the predominant color, and the vast majority of the women's hair was varying hues of blonde, as if they'd exchanged their Dulaney school uniforms for the uniforms of middle age.

"You've let your hair go gray," Helen said, as if reading Loretta's mind. "And you've grown it so long! Gosh, Loretta, I never thought I'd see you at a Dulaney reunion. Your parents don't still live on Silvan Lane, do they?"

"They moved to Florida over twenty years ago," Loretta said. She was about to add that both of them had passed away when she was silenced by the tinging of metal against glass.

The director of alumnae affairs made a dreary speech about tradition and friendship and academic excellence, at the end of which she urged everybody to consider donating money to the school. Loretta shook her head. "I can think of a million better causes than new tennis courts for a girls' school."

A woman sat down in the seat on the other side of Loretta. Her smile was more of a grimace, yellowed teeth and rubber band lips. She smelled strongly of an expensive lily-scented perfume that Loretta recognized as a scent she'd worn herself years ago, when it was the latest thing.

"It's a new library, actually," the woman said. "I'm head of the fund-raising committee."

"In that case, I'll write you a check," Loretta said, not intending to do any such thing. She looked longingly at her chicken salad. She'd driven up from New York that morning and hadn't eaten breakfast because of a nervous stomach.

"Loretta, don't you remember me?" the woman said. Loretta studied her.

"Janet!" she said. "Of course. But your hair is different, isn't it?"

"We were delighted when we heard you were coming," Janet said. "You'll be at the party tonight, I hope."

"Wouldn't miss it for the world," Loretta said. Who is *we*? Had she been talked about? By whom, and what had they said? She'd never much liked Janet, who'd been the captain of the field hockey team. Loretta had sung in the *a cappella* group, which had its own cachè. She knew from the Paperless Post she'd received that the party would be at Janet's house. She imagined orange slices offered around on aluminum trays, as they had been at field hockey games.

"Do you still do art?" Helen said.

Do art? Loretta thought. As in *do* needlework, or *do* decoupage? "Yes, I'm an installation artist," she said.

Helen smiled and nodded as if she knew what an installation artist was. Loretta doubted it. No, that was unfair, she told herself; she knew nothing about Helen anymore.

"There is an exhibit of my work in a gallery in Manhattan

right now. My pieces are on exhibit all over the world, actually."

"The world!" Helen said. "My goodness."

Loretta smiled. "Yes, it's exciting. At the moment I'm working on a commission for the Hamburger Bahnhof in Berlin." She had a plan on paper that involved plastic domes and roaming lights, but she kept putting off researching materials for fear the mechanics of it wouldn't work. She'd won the commission over a more important artist, and her fear of failure was so intense that it kept her up at night.

"And what does your husband do?" Helen said.

"My husband?" Loretta said. "I don't have a husband."

Helen looked perplexed. "You never married? Why did I think you had?"

"Oh, I've been married," Loretta said. "I'm just not married right now."

"Ah," Helen said. "Thought so."

"Thrice," Loretta said. She held up three fingers and took a sip from a goblet of white wine. "Once to a man much older than me, and once to a man much younger, and once to a man exactly my age, in fact our birthdays fell on the same day."

"That sounds like a riddle or a fairy tale," Helen said. "You must have a pack of children."

"What makes you think that?" Loretta said.

"I don't know," Helen said. "Three husbands. Men always want children, not that they take care of them."

"I don't like children," Loretta said, though this wasn't true, it was simply an easy excuse for not having any that tended to shut people up. She'd given birth to a stillborn baby when she was thirty-four, a girl who would have been on the cusp of adolescence had she lived. The husband whose birthday she shared, an archeologist named Ben, had been the father of that baby. She had left her much older first husband for him and had already been pregnant when they married.

"I don't like them either," Helen said. "But I ended up having twin boys. They were perfect monsters when they were little. They're grown up now, thank God."

Loretta laughed. "So what do you do?"

"Me?" Helen said. "Nothing much. I read a lot. I like to putter in the garden." She looked at Loretta with untroubled blue eyes. "My husband runs a hedge fund. Do you know what that is?"

"Sure," Loretta said.

"Oh, good," Helen said. She resettled herself in her chair and speared a piece of chicken with her fork. "Because I couldn't begin to explain it to you. All I know is he makes pots of money. I haven't worked since my boys were born."

"Don't you want to work?" Loretta said, trying not to sound judgmental.

"Why would I want to work when I can afford not to?"

Loretta shrugged. "For the satisfaction of it maybe?"

"Maybe," Helen said. "But I can't imagine what I would do."

Loretta gazed around the room, recognizing the forty-eight-year-old versions of girls she used to know. She hoped she looked better than most of them. Delia Hart had gained at least fifty pounds, and Amanda Keener's facelift made her look like an ancient feline. Helen looked much the same as she had at school, only stouter, blonder, and oddly imploded-looking, like a month-old jack o' lantern.

"Helen, where is Barbara?" she said. "I don't see her here."

"Oh, dear," Helen said. "Didn't you hear? No, you wouldn't have. Barbara died last year."

"What?" Loretta said. "No."

Helen nodded. "Lydia Heffender passed away last year as well, and Karen Petit the year before."

"But how?" Loretta said.

"Cancer," Helen said. "Breast, pancreatic, endometrial. And Kathy Garvey dropped dead of a brain aneurism about five years ago. We're getting old, Loretta."

"Not that old! Not *dying* old."

"This is how I look at it," Helen said. "It's not a matter of *if* I get some awful illness anymore, now it's a matter of *when*."

"That's a terrible attitude," Loretta said. "I refuse to think like that."

"It's been thirty years," Helen said. "Hard to believe, isn't it?" She tapped Loretta's wine glass with her own. "Cheers. What do you say we get stinking drunk?"

"God yes, let's do," Loretta said gloomily.

"I'm joking, Loretta!" Helen said. "If I drank more than a glass of wine at lunch I'd fall asleep for the rest of the day."

Loretta nodded and dug into her salad. "Of course you would," she said.

A mile of pea gravel led through a forest of oaks before the landscape opened up and Janet's house came into view. Loretta, running late and feeling lost, almost turned back halfway there, but the GPS said she was on the right track, so she decided to trust it rather than herself. She wouldn't have imagined that Janet lived so far out of town; one of those stalwart colonials on Main Street seemed more her style. But the house was even larger than any on Main, a shingled pile at the edge of a pond.

"Loretta!" someone called as soon as she walked in. A brittle blonde woman and a completely bald man seemed delighted to see her.

"Hello!" Loretta said. She couldn't recall the woman's name. Penny? Patsy? Something with a P.

"Jake, darling, do you remember Loretta?" the woman said to the man.

"Loretta! Of course I remember you!" he said.

"You do?" Loretta said. She'd never seen him before in her life.

"Loretta!" another voice called. "*Here* you are." It was Janet, wearing a floral caftan and a chunky green statement necklace— her idea of dressy, Loretta thought. Loretta wore a black satin skirt and a simple cream blouse, her hair curling loose down her back. Janet led Loretta to a large room whose windows overlooked the pond. Flutes of champagne were arranged on a table in military rows. Loretta accepted one.

"Loretta," said Helen, squeezing by a portly man in a business suit. She caught the arm of a passing woman. "Do you remember Tabitha Peters?"

Tabitha had sung *a cappella* as well. She'd been a chubby girl and was a heavy-set woman, her once-brown hair now auburn.

"You've kept your figure, I'm jealous," Tabitha said. She squeezed her stomach, a handful of fat. "Oh well. I couldn't be bothered."

A maid came by and exchanged Loretta's empty champagne glass for a full one. She had nothing to say to Tabitha. She'd completely forgotten her until now.

"Where is the bathroom?" she said, simply to get away. The room was crowded and growing hot. There was an oniony smell of invisible hors d'oeuvres, and somebody's husband was wearing too much cologne.

Helen pointed. "Down the hall, take a right. You'll know you're close when you get a whiff of chlorine. Janet had a lap pool installed back there."

"A lap pool?" Loretta said.

"You know, one of those pools that has a current you swim against."

"I've never heard of that," Loretta said.

"Seriously?" Helen said. "It's something to see." She beckoned with her forefinger. Loretta followed her out into the foyer and down a long hall whose carpeting was so deep that she felt herself sink with every step. When the odor of chlorine reached them, Helen turned left and opened a door. She flipped a switch in the wall and row of lights in the ceiling came on. Beside the light switch were a larger switch and a round thermostat. The room was long and narrow; the back wall was almost all glass, framing a well-tended garden that was striped by the last rays of the sun. A small rectangular swimming pool was sunk into the floor.

"You can't do laps in that," Loretta said.

"No, look," Helen said, and flipped the larger switch. Somewhere behind the wall, a motor hummed and the water in the pool began to ripple as if blown by a steady wind. "That's the current. I've tried swimming against it and it's plenty strong. So you can swim every day without having to put in a big pool. Great idea, huh?"

Loretta considered the pool before answering. "It's the

aquatic equivalent of a stationary bike. You move without going anywhere."

"The idea isn't to go anywhere, it's to keep fit," Helen said.

Loretta imagined Janet's arms wheeling, her legs kicking up a froth, while the current kept her body prisoner. "I think it's creepy, to tell you the truth."

"You were always a naysayer," Helen said with a smile.

"Helen, why did you ask me what my husband does immediately after I told you about myself?" Loretta said. The conversation had nagged at her all afternoon as she lay around in her hotel room.

"Just curious," Helen said.

"More curious about my husband than about me?"

"No," Helen said. "I always ask people what their spouses do."

"Okay. Can you remember what I told you about myself?"

"Yes, of course. You said you're an artist. You're doing something in Germany."

"That's a sketch of it, I guess."

"You wanted to impress me," Helen said. "It was obvious and it annoyed me. That's really why I asked what your husband did, to be honest, to get you off the subject of yourself."

"You *asked* me about myself," Loretta said. "What did you expect me to say?"

"I just hate braggarts," Helen said. "You were always a little conceited."

"That's not true!" Loretta said. "Don't tell me you weren't bragging when you said your husband makes pots of money."

"That's different," Helen said. "I wasn't talking about myself." She flipped the switch to the pool's motor and the room went quiet. "The bathroom is across the hall."

She turned off the lights and they left the room. Loretta went into the bathroom and sat on the toilet for several minutes before someone knocked on the door. Jake was there when she came out.

"Loretta," he said. "I thought I saw you come back here."

Loretta put her hand to her chest. "You're looking for me?"

"You know, I always admired you," he said. "Back when you were at Dulaney." He chuckled and scratched his freckled head. "You were way too cool to notice me. Look at you! You're just as gorgeous as you were then."

"I don't think I was gorgeous. Or cool. But thank you all the same." All of a sudden she did remember Jake. She'd been aware of his admiration. She recalled having rudely turned down his invitation to a mixer at his school. *In your dreams*, she had said. She blushed now to think about it. She must have thought she was something special to be that nasty to a boy.

"Well," Jake said. He dug his hands into his pockets. "If you don't mind."

"Oh, excuse me," she said, stepping out of his way. He actually needed to use the bathroom; he hadn't been looking for her after all.

"This is what I want to know," Tabitha said. She and Loretta sat on the bottom step of a flight of stairs that led to the second floor. Neither woman was entirely sober. Tabitha had been a cozy, confiding girl at school. She hadn't changed, Loretta thought. "Why *this* class reunion, after all these years? You never came to one before."

"I'm a successful artist now," Loretta said. "Which, by the way, is no easy thing to achieve. But no one cares about that. I've been asked several times where my husband is, though, and how many children I have."

"I have three," Tabitha said. "Two boys and a girl. They are the lights of my life. I never had a career, but being a mother has been so rewarding." She clasped her hands and looked at the ceiling, as if thanking God for the experience.

"I had a baby girl, but she died," Loretta said. A day didn't pass that she didn't think about her daughter, but she'd never spoken about her before. Losing her was a tragedy more painful and private than any in her life, yet here she was almost boasting about it in a game of maternal one-upmanship.

"Oh, how terrible," Tabitha said. "I'm so sorry, Loretta, I can't tell you how sorry. Nothing is worse than losing a child."

"I've never gotten over it," Loretta said. She'd known the baby was dead before she'd given birth. She had slid out after a short labor, perfect and gray, and Loretta had held her to her chest. Warm from Loretta's womb, eventually her wet skin cooled. The nurse had looked at Loretta with sorrow; the doctor had already left the room. "You have to give her up now," Ben had whispered. Loretta named her Clementine, as she and Ben had planned. Not long afterward, she left him, which she came to regret. But she'd had to hold someone accountable for her misery, and he was who she blamed.

"And here I was envying you because you're so youthful and thin," Tabitha said. She sighed. "Everyone has a cross to bear."

"Maybe," Loretta said. "Though some people's lives seem pretty great." She looked at Janet's stairway wall, where a dozen photographs recorded decades of family life. When Janet was on her deathbed, it would be standing room only. Loretta would die alone.

"Am I the only single, childless woman in our class?" she said.

"There's Mary Butler," Tabitha said. "She's a lesbian. No, wait. I think I heard she got married."

A lightening crack of pain flashed behind Loretta's eyes. She put her champagne glass on the floor. This was what happened when she'd had too much to drink. "I need an aspirin," she said as she got to her feet.

"Try Janet's room," Tabitha said. "First door off the landing on the left."

Loretta went up the stairs to Janet's bathroom, where she opened the mirrored cabinet over the sink. There were the usual items, Advil, Gas-X, dental floss, and several prescription vials. Loretta read the label on one. *Klonazapam, 1mg. As needed.* So, Janet was anxious; Loretta would never have guessed. She opened the vial, tipped a tablet onto her palm, and slid it into the pocket of her skirt. She had taken Klonazapam after the baby; three of them made her sleep through the day.

She went into Janet's extremely pink bedroom—gingham upholstery, flowered wallpaper, the same garden view as from the lap pool—and sat on the edge of the bed. She took her phone from her purse and scrolled through her contact list. The number she had was for a landline. Who used those anymore? The last time they'd spoken was ten years ago, before the short-lived mistake of her third marriage. She tapped the number with her thumb and put the phone to her ear. The call went immediately to an automated voice asking her to leave a message. She paused before speaking.

"Ben, it's Loretta," she said. "I hope this is still you. I was thinking about us. I was remembering Clementine. The funny thing is I miss her. I didn't even know her, but I miss her every day, even after all these years. Do you ever think about her, Ben? Do you think about us?" It probably wasn't even Ben's number anymore; she might be baring her soul to a stranger. "This sounds strange, or maybe it doesn't, but sometimes I think Clementine is with me. I sense her by my shoulder, sort of a warm weight, as if she's leaning on me. It's nice, I like it; she makes me feel less alone." She swiped her wet cheek with her fist. "I wanted her so badly, more than anything in the world. Sometimes I imagine that Clementine is alive, and you and I are together. Do you remember going to Woodstock the summer I was pregnant? We talked about buying a house. We thought we'd have a child soon, but then we didn't and everything was ruined."

There was a clattering sound on the line and then a little girl's voice. "Hello?"

"Oh, I'm sorry," Loretta said. She looked around for a Kleenex. There was a box on Janet's nightstand. "I thought this was Ben Silver's number."

"He isn't here right now," the girl said. "Do you want to talk to my mom?"

"Your mom?" Loretta said. "Who are you?"

"Sophie," the girl said.

"Sophie," Loretta said. Sophie was Ben's grandmother's name. "How old are you, Sophie?"

"Eight," Sophie said. "How old are you?"

"Would you do me a favor and erase my message?" Loretta said. "Do you know how to do that?"

"Yes," Sophie said. "I can do that."

"Thanks," Loretta said, and hung up.

Her anonymous hotel room beckoned, a fresh-smelling pillow and a Klonazapam slumber. She gathered her bag and wrap and decided to say goodbye to Helen. She found her with Janet's maid in the kitchen, replenishing the champagne.

"I'm helping out," Helen said.

"You were my best friend," Loretta said. "You and Barbara."

"We had fun back then, didn't we?" Helen said. She dried a flute with a dish towel and carefully put it on the counter by the sink. The maid was refilling the clean ones from a large bottle of champagne.

"I guess we did," Loretta said. "The world was so different in those days. But I wanted to say goodbye to you. I doubt I'll see you again."

Helen frowned. "Have you been crying?"

"Yes," Loretta said.

"But why?" Helen said. "I thought things were going so well for you."

"Bad things have happened in my life," Loretta said.

"Bad things happen in everybody's lives," Helen said.

Loretta watched the maid arrange the glasses on a tray. "I shouldn't have come. It was stupid of me."

Helen put down the dishrag. "I know you think we're all dumpy and conventional, Loretta, but our lives are every bit as important as yours."

"I didn't say they weren't," Loretta said. "That's not what I was thinking."

"Then what were you thinking," Helen said flatly.

"That my life is different, that's all."

Helen made a disparaging sound. "Arty Loretta, the class bohemian."

Loretta traced the swirling pattern in the marble countertop with her fingertip, trying to come up with the right thing to say. She couldn't remember what she'd been thinking when she decided to come to the reunion. "I've worked so hard, you have no idea," she said. "Ambition. It's useless, really."

"You're drunk," Helen said. "You're slurring your words." She turned back to the sink and took up washing glasses again. Loretta lingered behind her.

"I didn't get what I wanted if that makes you feel any better," she said. Helen stopped washing and turned off the tap with an abrupt twist of her hand.

"Now, why would that make me feel better," she said. "Why would it make me feel anything at all?"

Loretta stepped away from her. "I was trying to tell you about my life."

"You know what?" Helen said. "You're right, you shouldn't have come." She looked at Loretta's wrap and bag. "It seems you're leaving anyway."

"I just wanted to say goodbye to you, Helen. That's all I came in here to do."

"Goodbye, then," Helen said.

The party was in full swing as Loretta waded back into it. It would go late, she guessed, and be much discussed the next day. She inched past clots of chatting classmates, catching snippets of conversations. But nobody tried to talk to her. No one asked her to stay.

Let Me Stay with You

Ripley could see Freddy waiting for him on the other side of passport control, his friend's familiar silhouette dim and wavering beyond the smeared glass barrier.

"At last!" Freddy said as Ripley came through the exit, his suitcase gliding behind him. "Claire can't wait to see you. She's cooking up a feast."

"Terrific, I'm starving," Ripley said. Claire was French on her mother's side and cared about food; Freddy's belly was evidence of that. Ripley had lost weight since his wife left him, eating deli soups and salads instead of making proper meals. He liked the idea of being fed and was looking forward to sleeping in an unfamiliar bed.

They walked out into the blazing day. Freddy's Fiat was in a nearby lot. As they drove out of the airport and took the *autoroute* past the industrial outskirts of Toulouse, he said, "We've got someone else visiting, our friend Bob. But don't worry, he's very independent. Spends most of the day by the pool."

"Why would I be worried?" Ripley said.

"I don't know," Freddy said. "Maybe you wanted to be here alone."

"I've been alone for a month," Ripley said. Freddy didn't reply. So they weren't going to talk about Kate. Ripley wondered if Bob had been briefed. *Ripley's wife ran off with another man*, he imagined Claire saying. *Ran off* was how she would put it. He could see her shrugging. *C'est la vie.* That nobody truly cared about the fracture of his marriage had come as another unwelcome surprise.

After an hour, Freddy turned off onto a rutted road. The dark cones of cypress trees on either side made Ripley think of Roman soldiers.

"Welcome to the middle of nowhere!" Freddy said in a jolly voice. "I'm afraid we've lured you to the least fashionable area of France."

"But it's beautiful here," Ripley said. The landscape was severe and rocky, as arid as it appeared from the plane. Golden-brown hills looked like the backs of sea lions and were speckled with twisted shrubs. Freddy and Claire's house was a three-story rectangle, ochre stucco over stone. Casement windows opened out, revealing sheer curtains lifting in the breeze. A giant tree that Ripley couldn't identify cast an ellipse of shade on the lawn, and a long table beneath it was set for a meal. Claire came out of the house.

"Ripley, how wonderful!" she said. She hugged him tightly. "I've made a cassoulet for lunch. I hope you like rabbit."

"Who doesn't like rabbits?" Ripley said, and she laughed. She was a tiny woman, very thin and neat. Freddy and Ripley had known her slightly at college; she and Freddy met again later on. They had a teenaged daughter, Elise. Though they lived in Manhattan, they spent August and Christmastime in France.

Freddy took Ripley's suitcase and led him into the house. It was dim and cool and smelled faintly of burnt wood; the living room fireplace was large enough to roast a couple of goats. Ripley's room was at the top of a narrow flight of stone stairs. He looked at the photographs on the stairwell wall, snaps of Freddy and Claire when they were younger, pictures of Elise at every age, and an old black and white of a glamorous-looking couple, somebody's grandparents, he assumed. His bedroom was beneath the eaves, with an old-fashioned brass double bed and a bookcase full of paperbacks. He wondered if this was the bedroom he would have been given had he and Kate arrived together.

"It's the only bedroom on this floor," Freddy said. "Plenty of privacy, and you've got your own bath." He opened a door to a small white tiled bathroom where there was a miniature sink and a toilet and shower. "Believe me, it's a luxury. Bob and Elise have to share a bathroom."

"It's great," Ripley said. "Thanks so much." He looked out the window at a long swimming pool, its surface reflecting a small fair weather cloud.

"Well, I'll leave you to unpack," Freddy said. When Ripley turned, his friend was gone.

He lay down on the bed and stared at the ceiling. He supposed he should wash up and reappear downstairs. He could hear voices through the open window, a man's deep-throated laugh. "I don't *want* to," he heard a girl's voice complain. Then Claire: "That's just too bad." Somebody stomped into the room beneath him. A few moments later, Elise appeared at his door.

"Hi, Uncle Ripley."

He sat up on his elbows. "Hey, Elise. Wow, you've grown up." The last time he saw her she'd had braces on her teeth and was several inches shorter. She had breasts now, and a scattering of pimples on her forehead. He wouldn't have predicted she'd end up being pretty, but she was, very, with her mother's brown curls and her father's blue eyes, and somebody else's long legs. "You're too old now to call me uncle, especially as I'm not your uncle. Just call me Ripley.

"Okay, Ripley. Can I take a shower in your bathroom?" She held up a loofah. "I wouldn't ask, but Bob is hogging my bathroom, his stuff is all over the place."

"Sure, go ahead," Ripley said.

"You're the best," she said. He lay back down and listened to the water running. When the water stopped, he heard Elise humming.

"Clean as a whistle?" he asked when she came out. She rubbed a towel over her damp hair and regarded him solemnly.

"Mom says Aunt Kate left you."

"She did," Ripley said.

"That sucks," Elise said.

"You have no idea," Ripley said.

"Dad said we're not to talk about it, but I don't think that's fair."

"Fair?" Ripley said.

"To you," Elise said. "When my boyfriend broke up with me last winter, I wanted to talk about how I felt all the time. But maybe you don't, I don't know."

"I do," Ripley said. "But I've run out of people to talk to."

"Well, you can talk to me whenever you want," Elise said. "I totally understand."

"Thank you, Elise, that's nice," Ripley said.

After she left, he took a shower. The bathroom was redolent of her fruity shampoo. He went downstairs and joined Freddy and Bob at the table beneath the tree. Bob was an architect at a big firm in Manhattan. His striped linen shirt looked so crisp and fresh that Ripley thought it must have been brand new.

"I'm an architect too," Ripley told him. "I have my own firm in Greenwich."

"Freddy told me. Residential, I assume," Bob said, looking at Ripley over the rims of his fashionably round glasses.

"I've never been intrigued by office buildings," Ripley said mildly. Bob raised his eyebrows and looked away.

Claire carried the cassoulet out from the kitchen in a pair of oven mitts. Elise followed her with a basket of bread. Freddy popped open a bottle of red wine. He raised his glass and cleared his throat.

"Here's to Ripley's very welcome presence."

Ripley smiled and touched Freddy's glass with his own. If Kate hadn't left him, he wouldn't have come.

Ripley knew, or knew of, most of Freddy's friends, but he'd never heard of Bob.

"We haven't known him long," Freddy said. "He's actually more of an acquaintance, a friend of a friend in New York. He said he would be in Paris on business and hinted he'd like to visit, so we thought why not, and invited him down for a few days. He seems very nice." They were sitting on the patio at the back of the house. Bob lay in a chaise next to the pool, tan and lean and wearing green floral swim trunks, looking like a magazine ad. Elise swam back and forth with a maximum of splashing. When she stopped swimming and got out of the pool, Ripley noticed Bob staring at her as she dried herself with a towel. The wet bottom of her bikini sagged, exposing a tender pale inch of her ass. She twisted around and patted her back with the towel, then bent to dry her legs. Finally, she wrapped the towel around her body, and Bob went back to the book he was reading. Ripley let out a breath.

"I suppose he's gay," Freddy said.

"No," Ripley said.

"It's kind of obvious," said Freddy. "I mean, look at him, he's impeccable."

"I don't like him," Ripley said.

Freddy looked at Ripley with surprise. "But you like everybody. It's one of your best qualities. I've never heard you say a bad word about anyone."

Ripley shrugged. "I'm going for a hike." He went to change. He'd been warned about ticks, so he put on long pants and took his baseball cap to wear against the sun. There was a knock at his door. It was Elise again, loofah in hand.

"The problem is," she began.

"You hate sharing a bathroom with Bob," Ripley said. "Please, be my guest."

"The door doesn't lock properly, and I feel like he might barge in any second. I'm being silly, I know."

"No, you're not," Ripley said.

He set out on a trail that led through the brush to a promontory overlooking a small lake. Iridescent ducks floated around emerald isles of algae; sparrows flitted and swooped. A family of turtles lazed on a log—Ripley counted eight—and every now and then a fish would rise and kiss the surface for a breath of air. A weeping willow leaned as if knocked over by a storm, its whip-thin branches shadowing the water. Someone had put a wooden bench under an apple tree. Ripley sat down and covered his eyes with his hands. The breeze was hot as a furnace. When he'd woken up that morning, he'd wanted to go home so badly he felt physically sick, but getting there seemed so complicated, the journey so long, that he fell back against the pillows. He'd heard noises in the house, smelled coffee and bacon; he waited for Freddy to summon him to breakfast. But nine o'clock passed, then ten. He put on his clothes and crept down the stairs.

"Good morning!" Claire said, and handed him a cup of coffee. "We thought it best to let you sleep. Sit down, have a croissant."

Ripley took a small bite of the pastry. "This is delicious," he said. "The coffee too."

"Of course they are, you're in France," Claire said cheerfully, and Ripley thought then that he'd be all right.

But now he felt the bleakness returning. He would be miserable wherever he was, but here he felt he had to pretend to be happy not to make the others feel awkward.

"Are you crying?"

He took his hands away from his face. Elise. Her damp hair darkened the shoulders of her T-shirt. She was holding a book to her chest. "You're everywhere, aren't you?" he said.

"I come here to read sometimes. But you've got dibs. I'll leave you alone."

"No, stay," Ripley said. "I could use the company."

"You were thinking about Aunt Kate," Elise said as she sat down on the bench. "Dad said he wasn't surprised about Aunt Kate, that she's super intense and it was only a matter of time before she went off the rails somehow. You were in love, weren't you?"

"Madly," Ripley said.

Elise nodded. "It's sort of exhausting being in love, don't you think? It takes a lot of energy. And then you break up and there's nowhere to put it."

Ripley looked at her. Shadow and light dappled her face, framed by the apple tree's browning leaves. "Exactly," he said. "Sometimes I feel as if I'm going to explode."

"That's why you have to talk about it. It's like you're a balloon and you need to let out air." She pursed her lips and blew out a peppermint breath. "When my boyfriend broke up with me, my mom sent me to a therapist."

"Really," Ripley said. "That seems kind of extreme."

"My therapist says you can't judge yourself for your feelings," she said.

"I'm not judging," he said.

"Therapy really helped. I'd consider it if I were you."

"I just might," Ripley said. "How old are you again?"

"Fourteen."

She opened her book and began to read. He sat looking out at the lake. A white heron flew down to the top of the willow. A yellow butterfly alighted on his knee. He couldn't decide if Kate would like it here. In general, she didn't care for traveling, but she had always enjoyed seeing Claire. He wondered if he would find someone again, then shut his eyes to erase the idea. If he thought about a future without her, it was an admission that she wasn't coming back. Instead, he imagined her waiting for him when he flew into JFK, except she didn't know he was away.

After a while, Elise took her cellphone out of her pocket and looked at the time. "One thirty," she said, closing her book. "Lunchtime. We're having roast chicken. There's nothing like French chicken, you know."

"No, I didn't know," Ripley said. Together, they walked back down the trail, helping each other when the rocks got tricky. When they emerged from the brush, Claire and Freddy and Bob were already at the table. When Claire looked at Ripley he felt as if he were in trouble.

"So, what have *you* two been up to?" Bob said as Ripley and Elise sat down.

"Hanging out," Elise said. "Reading. Talking."

"Talking about what?" Freddy said.

"About love," Ripley said. "Bob, I'm sure Claire and Freddy told you that my wife recently left me. I'm afraid she's pretty much all I can think about right now. Elise is a good listener."

"Elise," Claire said impatiently.

"I don't think a grown man should talk to a child about love," Freddy said.

"First of all, I'm not a child," Elise said. "Secondly, why not?" Freddy balked. "See, you can't think of a reason."

Freddy looked intently at Ripley. Claire said something in French to Elise.

"The chicken looks good," Bob said.

"There's nothing like French chicken," Ripley said as Claire sliced the meat from the bone.

After lunch, Ripley went up to his room to take a nap. Though he'd been dead tired the night before, he hadn't slept very well, waking every hour or so. He lay down on the bed and dozed. When he started awake thirty minutes later, his shirt was damp with sweat. He knew he'd been dreaming but he couldn't remember what about. He never remembered his dreams. Kate use to tease him about it, saying not remembering meant he was emotionally repressed. Dreams, she said, were the keys to the unconscious mind, and she claimed that hers were often prophetic. She was interested in anything that had to do with prophesy—palmistry, Tarot cards, runes—and regularly consulted an astrologer she'd known since before she and Ripley met. He thought about what Freddy said, that it was only a matter of time before Kate went off the rails. It made Ripley feel better, Freddy's putting it like that.

He rose and splashed his face at the sink. What he needed was a swim. He went to the window to see if Bob was still lazing by the pool. He was. Elise was there as well, sunbathing in another chaise. Bob squeezed sunblock out of a tube and rubbed it across his chest. He pointed the tube at Elise and said something. Elise shrugged in response. Bob got up and sat on the end of her chaise.

"Don't," Ripley said as she squirted a blob of cream on Bob's back. When she handed back the tube after a cursory effort at spreading the sunblock around, Bob made a circular motion with his finger. Elise jackknifed her knees to her chest and spun around in a single movement. Bob straddled the chaise behind her. Horrified, Ripley watched him massage Elise's shoulders. He said something that made Elise laugh, then slid his hands to her lower back.

Ripley put on his swim trunks and grabbed a towel from

the bathroom. He nearly fell as he ran down the steps. Freddy stood in the hall.

"There you are," he said. He jingled some change in the pocket of his shorts. "Listen, could we have a chat?"

"Sure," Ripley said, draping the towel around his neck. "But I think we should go out to the pool."

"No, I'd rather talk here," Freddy said. He gazed somewhere past Ripley's left ear. "It's about Elise. I know she seems precocious, but she's really quite naïve. I'd prefer it if you would…" He looked at Ripley. "Well, I hate to put it bluntly, but I want you to leave her alone."

"Leave her alone?" Ripley said. Then he realized what Freddy meant. "You think I'm coming on to Elise? No way, Freddy, I would never do that."

"I hope that's so," Freddy said. "But I don't think it's appropriate for a grown man to talk about his personal problems with an impressionable young woman. I realize Elise is very attractive—"

"Listen," Ripley said. "It's not me you have to worry about. It's Bob. He openly ogles Elise. I just saw him massaging her back, for God's sake. Do you think *that's* appropriate?"

"Oh, come on, Ripley, Bob is gay."

"How do you know?" Ripley said. "Did he tell you?"

"He doesn't have to!" Freddy said.

Ripley shook his head. "You're wrong."

"Anyway," Freddy said, exhaling the word. "I'm sorry I had to say it, but I thought it needed to be said."

"Okay," Ripley said. "You've been heard."

"I mean it," Freddy said.

"I know you do." He started to go out to the pool. Then he stopped. "Maybe I should go home tomorrow."

"There's no reason for that," Freddy said. "Unless you really feel you must."

With a pang, Ripley saw he was relieved.

Having poured himself a glass of scotch from Freddy's bar, Ripley sat out on the patio while the sky turned pink and the shadow of the house slid over the pool. In the kitchen, Claire and Bob and Elise were making pizzas for dinner. "I thought we were in France, not Italy!" he heard Bob say. "They're *French* pizzas," Elise said. It was clear that Freddy hadn't told anyone that Ripley would be leaving.

Elise came out with a bowl of olives. "Come inside?" she said. "We're having fun."

"The air is so soft," Ripley said. He took an olive. "I'm enjoying myself out here."

"Well, dinner's almost ready," she said sternly. He thought she might order him to wash his hands. "We're eating in the kitchen." She pointed up at a filmy bank of scalloped clouds. "Do you know what that cloud formation is called?"

"A mackerel sky," Ripley said.

She huffed her annoyance. "I didn't think anyone else knew that," she said. "I read it in my book."

Ripley chuckled. "Whatever you know, someone else knows it too. Think of the most unimaginable thing you can tell me. Let's see if you can shock me."

"I'll have to think about it," she said. "Can I tell you later?

"Take your time," he said.

Freddy came out to the patio. "What are you two talking about?" he said.

"Uncle Ripley wants me to shock him," Elise said.

"Elise, darling, set the table, will you?" Freddy said. When she was gone, he said, "What the hell, Ripley."

"No, Freddy, you misunderstood. We were talking about facts. I asked her to think of a fact I don't know."

"How is it that I always misunderstand?" Freddy said.

"I don't know," Ripley said. "But you do. Why don't you ask her?"

"She's just a kid, Ripley."

"Whatever," Ripley said. He spit an olive pit into his hand. Explaining was hopeless, he realized.

A few minutes later, he heard Claire call his name. He went into the kitchen for dinner. Freddy didn't look at Ripley as he handed him a plate of pizza. So, all was lost, Ripley thought sadly. They had been friends for twenty-six years.

He tapped his wine glass with his fork. "I'd like to make a toast," he said. "Freddy, Claire, thank you for your friendship. I love you both."

"Oh, my goodness," Claire said. "We haven't even opened a second bottle and you're already being maudlin."

"Let's open one then," Freddy said.

Pleading jet lag, Ripley excused himself soon after dinner. He lay on his bed reading a paperback mystery until he felt tired, then took one more sleeping pill than the label on the vial prescribed. There would be hours to think on the flight home, but he didn't want to think tonight. He fell into a heavy black sleep but was dragged back into the pallor of consciousness seemingly a moment later. Elise was saying his name. She stood by the side of his bed.

"What is it?" Ripley said. He looked at his phone. It was twenty past three. He'd been asleep for four hours.

"Can I sleep in here?" she said. "I won't be a bother. I'll sleep on the floor."

"What?" He turned on the bedside lamp and squinted against the glare. "Of course you can't, Elise. Go back to bed immediately." He sat up and really looked at her. She was hugging herself and trembling. "What is it? What's going on? Here, sit down." He moved over as she sat on the side of the bed, careful not to touch her.

"Bob came into my room," she whispered. "I was asleep, and then I woke up. He was in bed with me, Uncle Ripley."

"Oh, Jesus," Ripley said. "Did he do anything to you?"

She shook her head. "I got out of bed and ran up here. I'm scared. I don't want to go back."

"I don't blame you," he said. "Come on, let's wake your parents."

Elise grabbed his arm, a falcon's grip. "No, please."

"Why not?"

"Because. Today, at lunch? Mom called me *audacieux*, bold. She thinks I was flirting with you. I wasn't, was I?"

"No, of course not," Ripley said.

"I don't want to tell," she said.

"Then I will," Ripley said, and started to get out of bed.

"No!" Elise said. "I don't want anyone to know."

"But I know," he said.

"You're different."

"How so?"

"You're not fake like most grown-ups. Like Mom and Dad. They pretend everything is wonderful all the time, but nothing is wonderful every day, and sometimes it won't ever be wonderful. They close their bedroom door and fight, and they think I can't hear them. Then they come out and act like their world is perfect. Why? What's the point? Is pretending going to make them like each other any better? I mean, it's like nothing bad is allowed be spoken of, you know? If I told them about Bob, they'd probably say I'd been dreaming." Her blue eyes were wide, her skin was translucent; the pimples on her forehead were angrily red. It rocked him to think that Freddy and Claire didn't get along; they'd always seemed so well-suited. He'd never thought of marriage as a tenuous state. He'd trusted Kate up until the moment she confessed she had fallen for another man.

"I didn't know that about your parents," he said.

"Neither do I, really," Elise said. "Their voices are muffled, but I can tell they're yelling. Who knows what they're arguing about."

Ripley caught his reflection in the mirror opposite his bed. His hair looked like it had been blown sideways by a stiff wind, exposing a dime-size coin of pale scalp above his temple. "Kate and I never argued. I thought *we* were perfect."

"My therapist says nothing is perfect," she said.

"But, Elise, if you don't want to tell your parents, what do you expect me to do?"

She curled herself against the footboard of his bed. "Let me stay with you."

He waited until her eyes blinked shut and her breathing slowed to a rhythm, then got out of bed and made his way down the unlit stairway, the stones icy beneath his bare feet.

He looked into her bedroom. Her bed was empty, the white sheets rumpled and stark. In the living room, he sat in a chair by the massive fireplace and watched the windows grow pale. The quiet was so deep it rang in his ears; his smallest sounds—a sniff, a swallow—seemed enormously amplified. It was evening in Connecticut now. Kate would be getting ready for bed. He imagined her wearing her blue chenille robe with the enormous pink appliqued flowers, sipping her usual cup of herbal tea, though it was just as likely she was wearing nothing and having sex with her lover. While he'd been in France, he hadn't thought about her for minutes at a time. Eventually he'd forget her for hours, then days, weeks, months, until thoughts of her would be as remote as this place to which he would never return.

Pulling Toward Meanness

The chaises surrounding the hotel swimming pool were in such demand that Kim had to wake up at six o'clock in the morning to get dibs on a couple before they were all taken. There were scads of them, fifty at least, but by eight o'clock they'd all be loaded with people's stuff, magazines and tote bags and towels. Waking to the faint ping-ping of the alarm on her phone, she'd run down to the pool and dump sunblock and books on two adjacent chaises. Then she'd run back up to the room and get into bed, snuggle against Andrea's back and sleep until ten.

"God, isn't this fabulous?" Andrea said on their second day there as they sat beneath the beating Miami sun. "I wish we lived down here."

"You'd be tan all year round," Kim said. Andrea was an olive-skinned brunette; Kim was a redhead, freckled and fair. But it was Andrea's turn to choose their vacation—Kim had chosen Aspen last June—and she liked nothing better than to laze in the sun. Kim reapplied sunblock several times a day and wore a wide-brimmed hat. Andrea had hated the rusticity of the rented cabin in Aspen; they'd squabbled about it and gone home a day early.

A woman sitting in the chaise next to Kim's smiled at her and said, "Where are you girls from?"

"Connecticut," Kim said.

"I used to love taking vacations with my girlfriends," the woman said. She was old enough to be wearing a bathing suit with a skirt, even though she wasn't fat. She noticed Kim's wedding ring. "Oh, you're married! I bet your husbands are off playing golf. I've heard the course here is gorgeous."

"Actually, we're married to each other," Andrea said before Kim could answer. "Going on two years."

The woman blinked. "Well. Imagine that."

"Don't have to imagine it," said Andrea. She sat up. "We're expecting a baby as well." She patted her still-flat belly and lay down again.

"No kidding!" the woman said. Kim thought she'd go back to her magazine, but she put it down and looked at Kim. Her eyes were bright with interest.

"I know a few gay men," she said. "But I've never met a gay woman."

That you know of, Kim thought. "Where are you from?"

"Willing, Ohio," the woman said. "A speck of a town. How did you manage that?" She pointed at Andrea and touched her own belly. "Did you go to one of those banks?"

"You mean a *sperm* bank?" Andrea said loudly.

"Yes, we did," Kim said.

"I have nothing against it," the woman said. "Just curious. I'm for gay rights all the way."

Kim expected Andrea to make another crack, but Andrea had nodded off, as she often did these days. She was twelve weeks along. They had decided she would have the first child because she was older, thirty-three to Kim's twenty-seven, then Kim would give birth to the second. Kim wasn't sure she even wanted one, but it was too late now. "You'll fall in love with it once it's born," Andrea had said. "All new mothers do." Yet, biologically the baby wasn't Kim's, so who knew how she would feel.

"I'm Mary," the woman said. She gestured with her thumb at a man lying next to her. He was reading a paperback, paying them no attention. "That's my husband, Pete." She cupped her hand around her mouth and whispered, "He's more conservative than I am, if you know what I mean."

"I'm dying for a swim," Kim said. She took off her hat and walked to the edge of the pool. For all the people lying around it, there was hardly anyone in it. A sharp-nosed old man breast-stroked slowly past, and a little girl played by herself on the steps. A teenaged boy sprang off the diving board. Kim dove in and swam underwater to the shallow end, then turned against the wall and swam through the foggy blue toward the deep end. Halfway there, she saw something white on the bottom of the pool. She dove down, picked it up, and brought it to the surface. It was a torn shard of paper, waterlogged but intact, the typewritten words on it still sharp enough to be read.

> There's a side of me that keeps pulling toward meanness, I can't help myself. What is wrong with me?

Kim swam to the side of the pool and laid the paper on the hot cement. She squinted up at the balconies overlooking the pool and imagined the scrap of paper flying down like a feather.

"I'm hungry," Andrea called. "Baby needs a cheeseburger."

Kim climbed out of the pool. "Look what I found in the water."

Andrea held up the wet paper and squinted at it. "What in the world?"

"I know, strange isn't it?"

Andrea handed the paper back. "It's horrible, throw it away," she said. "Will you go get us some lunch?"

Kim went to the busy snack bar and ordered a couple of burgers. The deep shade beneath the snack bar's eave made waiting a pleasant reprieve. Beyond the pool, the beach stretched to the Atlantic; there were umbrellas and chairs set up near the shore for guests of the hotel to use. But Andrea hated the feel of the sand between her toes as much as she loved the sun. Kim watched her spread sunblock on her arms. She was beautiful, and the baby would be too because they'd chosen the sperm of a handsome man—a surgeon, like Andrea. When it was Kim's turn to have a baby would they choose *her* male counterpart, a wiry carrot-topped nurse? She smiled at the idea. In fact, they planned to use the same man's sperm so the children would be biologically related. This had been discussed before they married, when Kim had been so besotted with Andrea, she would have agreed to raise gorillas. Unconsciously, she frowned. Andrea could give birth to both babies as far as Kim was concerned: bearing witness to Andrea's various discomforts had put her off pregnancy entirely.

"No, no, no," Andrea said when Kim brought their lunch

over. "There are onions on this, you know I can't eat them." She peeled back the top bun and grimaced at her burger, which had been heaped with caramelized onions.

"So scrape them off," Kim said.

"I'll know they were there." She put her hand over her mouth. "Oh God, I feel like I'm going to vomit."

Kim took Andrea's plate, walked it back to the snack bar, and scraped the onions into a garbage can there. She waited a minute before returning to Andrea.

"Here you go," she said as she handed Andrea the plate.

"Fantastic," Andrea said. "What would I do without you?"

"It's a mystery," Kim said.

They sat on the balcony outside their room with a little table between them, eating toast and jam that room service had brought. Four floors down, their possessions covered two chaises by the pool. Kim watched a man and woman linger by the chaises and finally walk on. That's right, she thought, keep going.

"I had a dream about Jackson last night," she said.

"You mean a nightmare," Andrea said. She massaged her abdomen. "Speaking of which, I had the worst gas pains all night."

"He was telling me I was too stupid to be a doctor."

"I've told you a million times you would make an excellent doctor," Andrea said. "Why did you dream about him? Have you been thinking about him lately?"

Kim shook her head. "I never do." This wasn't entirely true, but true enough—she hardly ever thought about him. He had been her boyfriend senior year of college, just as her true sexuality was dawning on her. Perhaps he sensed that, or else he was just a prick, but a few months into their relationship, he'd become verbally abusive, denigrating her intellect and shaming her physically. He was the first real boyfriend she'd had, and she'd been reluctant to break up with him.

"It's that message you found in the pool yesterday," Andrea said. "It brought up bad memories, I bet."

"Maybe so," Kim said as she peeled open a tiny container of jam.

"You didn't keep it, I hope," Andrea said.

"No," Kim said. But she had. She'd slid it into the pocket of her tote bag, puckered and crisp from the sun.

"Yes, you did," Andrea said. "I hate it when you lie to me."

"I hate it when you tell me what to do," Kim said.

"I can't help it, I'm a doctor. It's my job to tell people what to do."

And it's my job to take orders from doctors, Kim thought. "I wish I'd never told you about Jackson," she said. Early in their relationship, Kim had laid herself at Andrea's feet by telling her every last thing about herself. Since then, she'd developed a habit of occasionally telling fibs in a small rebellion against Andrea's need to share every emotion and thought.

"What does Jackson have to do with my being bossy?" Andrea said.

"You're bossy to *me*," Kim said. "You think I'm weak because I let a man abuse me."

Andrea gave her a skeptical look. "You don't believe that. I don't think you're weak, you think you're weak. You've never forgiven yourself for staying with him."

She wasn't saying anything that Kim hadn't told her, but Kim felt as invaded as if her deepest secret had been unearthed. She rose from the table and went into the room, where the bed was a wreck of crumpled sheets. She found her tote bag, took the paper out of its pocket, and read it once again. She imagined it was a draft of a much longer letter that would be found after its author had packed up and gone. She regretted not breaking up with Jackson even more than she regretted their relationship; he had beaten her to the finish line and broken up with her, calling her a "waste of air" before he walked out the door. That she hadn't spat back a worse insult was another regret. She'd thought of dozens of comebacks since then.

She put the paper away just as Andrea came into the room.

"I'm sorry," she said. "Let's not fight. It's stupid to talk about Jackson, that was eons ago." She nuzzled Kim's neck and kissed the cleft between her breasts.

"Don't tell me you want to fool around during peak tanning hours," Kim teased. "What if someone takes our chaises?"

"They wouldn't dare," Andrea said. The curtains at the window inflated and collapsed with the breeze as Kim felt Andrea's mouth warm against her skin. Kim wondered if she had really been under Jackson's spell or simply desperate to prove that she was *normal*. Her parents had liked him. Doubtless they'd imagined she'd marry him, or someone like him, for they'd been deeply shocked when she came out. But she had a sister who was straight and married, and who had given them three grandchildren. Andrea and Kim's baby didn't count as a grandchild—Kim's mother had said as much. The father was anonymous, and the child wasn't related to Kim. She sighed and made a sound of pleasure, trying to empty her mind. Andrea took it so personally if Kim didn't enjoy herself that sometimes she felt compelled to pretend.

Kim reserved the same two chaises every morning because they were at the end of a row and faced the sun most of the day. A youngish couple sat where Mary and her husband had been the day before. The woman was blonde and chiseled in a crocheted bikini, her tanned body gleaming with lotion; the man wore a fashionable short growth of beard and a pair of tight red trunks that were almost as revealing as a Speedo.

"Did you bring the *Times*?" Kim heard the man say. "You forgot the *Times*, didn't you?" The woman sat up and handed him a large net bag.

"No, I didn't forget it."

"I couldn't see it under all your crap."

"Most of that 'crap' is yours," she said.

He reached into the bag and pulled out a *Vogue* magazine. "This isn't mine." He tossed it on the chaise at her feet. "And neither is this hairbrush."

"Two things," she said.

"I'm just proving a point. Your shit is in here too."

Kim leaned toward Andrea. "Are you listening to this?" she whispered.

"Trying not to," Andrea said.

"At least she's talking back to him," Kim said.

"Doesn't seem to make a difference."

Kim watched a couple of kids dive for pennies in the pool. She used to do that when she was a kid, except her father threw the pennies into the water and if she could retrieve them she got to keep them. They had been close until she came out, then something in him shut against her like a window against a wind. They were kind, her parents, but she had let them down. It didn't cross her mind that they had let *her* down until Andrea had pointed it out. "Being a parent means unconditionally loving your child," she'd said. But love was a variable thing, in Kim's opinion, it had layers that could be stripped off or worn away.

"Oh, for fuck's sake," said the man beside her. He held a tube of sunblock. "I need SPF 50 and this is only SPF 30."

Kim sat up and whispered in Andrea's ear. "I can't take this anymore. I'm going for a walk on the beach." But Andrea was asleep.

There was a gate in the wall that separated the pool area from the beach. Kim went through it and walked toward the shore, the sand tolerably hot beneath her feet. When she got to the water, she waded in up to her ankles and gazed out at a cruise ship on the horizon. Then she turned south and walked toward a distant cluster of skyscrapers, staying within the wet sand by the shore and looking fruitlessly for shells. She didn't see Mary until the woman was almost on top of her. She was wearing a different skirted bathing suit today, a snazzy red and black number. Yesterday Kim had figured her to be about her mother's age, but today she seemed younger. She held her graying hair against her head with one hand so the wind wouldn't blow it around. She was much taller than Kim, which hadn't been obvious when they'd been sitting in the chaises.

"Hello again! I've startled you! I was waving but you didn't see me. Are you looking for shells or thinking deeply?"

Kim laughed. "Shells, but there aren't any. Are you on your way back to the hotel?"

Mary looked at the water. "I wanted to take a swim, actually, but I don't like to swim alone. The water here is rough. Pete is golfing, he hates the beach."

"So does Andrea," Kim said. She assessed the waves, which were high and frothy, hitting the sand with a crash. "I'll swim with you, if you want."

"Oh, I don't want to disturb your walk," Mary said.

"I'm fleeing rather than walking," Kim said. "There's an awful couple sitting next to us that I'm trying to escape."

"More awful than I was?" Mary said with a smile. "I'm sorry I was so nosy yesterday. Pete says I talk too much. But I'm curious about people."

"Never mind, let's go in," Kim said. She took Mary's hand as they navigated the waves. The undertow was strong, and they held tight to each other until they were submerged in the chilly water. There were boys riding surfboards and children frolicking at the shore. The beach was crowded with hotel guests sitting beneath blue-and-white-striped umbrellas.

"I'm curious about people too," Kim said. "I'm a nurse, so I meet a lot of different types. Everyone has a story."

"I don't have much of one," Mary said. "I was married at twenty-two and had three boys by the time I was thirty. And I live in the most boring town in the country. Now, you're the one with a story. How long has gay marriage been legal?"

"Depends on the state," Kim said.

"Can I tell you a secret?" Mary said. "I always thought it would be nice to be with a woman." She blushed, which made Kim smile. They jumped as a wave came in, keeping their heads above water.

"It is nice," Kim said. "Very different than being with a man."

"Oh, men," Mary scoffed. "Men are such brutes."

"But you're married to one," Kim said.

"Barely." Mary rolled her eyes. "Watch out behind you!" she said.

A wave curled over Kim's head and crashed upon her, sucking her into its maw. She tried to swim to the surface but was pulled back down as if by a giant hand. She glimpsed Mary's legs for half a second, the skirt of her bathing suit floating above her pale thighs, then saw only a whirlwind of green water and sand.

Mary knelt over her, a dim silhouette. "You stopped breathing!" she said. "You almost drowned!"

"How?" Kim said, and then she remembered.

A man appeared opposite Mary. "Cough for me," he said. Kim coughed. Her chest felt like someone was sitting on it. She turned her head and vomited water. She touched a painful spot on her nose.

"It's not broken," Mary said. "Just scraped. Your arms and knees too. I had a time getting you out of the water. This man helped me, thank God, I didn't know what to do. He gave you CPR! He saved your life!"

"Thank you," Kim said.

"You're welcome," he said. He was older, white-haired, a little out of shape, not her idea of someone who could save a life. The bright sky behind him made her eyes throb. "We better get you to a hospital. Do you think you can walk?"

"I'll help you," Mary said.

Kim sat up. "No, I'm fine, I need to see Andrea. She's a doctor, she'll take care of me."

"I'm a doctor," the man said. "And I think you need to go to the hospital."

"Kim, come on," Mary said.

"No, no," Kim said. She got to her feet. "If Andrea thinks I should go, I will. I swear." She stumbled away from them, then vomited again. She knew the man was right, she needed medical attention, but she wanted to find Andrea.

"Here, let me take you," Mary said, putting her arm around Kim. The beach whirled and tilted; Kim stopped to cough several times. Mary rubbed her back in a circular motion. "Here we go, almost there." She opened the gate to the pool.

Two teenage girls attached by ear buds to their phones occupied Kim and Andrea's chaises.

"Excuse me," Mary said. One of them pulled out her ear

buds. "The woman who was here, do you know where she went?"

"There wasn't anyone here," the girl said.

"No, she wouldn't leave," Kim said.

"Well, she did," the girl said. "We got these chairs fair and square." She plugged her ear buds in again and went back to scrolling through her phone.

"All right, now I'm going to put my foot down," Mary said. "I'm driving you to the hospital."

Rudely, Kim shook her off and went to the door that led to the hotel elevator. Stepping into the elevator's mirrored interior, she saw that she was coated with sand. Her hair hung in clotted ropes, the scrape on her nose was deep; the whites of her eyes were entirely red, and her knees and forearms were raw. On the fourth floor, she got out and staggered down the carpeted hall, trailing sand behind her. Andrea had propped the door open with a book so Kim could get in without a key.

Andrea lay on the bed facing away from the door. She turned over as Kim walked in.

"I'm bleeding," she said.

"I almost drowned," Kim said.

Andrea began to cry. "I'm losing the baby," she said.

"I stopped breathing," Kim said. "I had to be revived."

"Don't you care about our baby?" Andrea said.

Kim didn't care; she never had. The baby was Andrea's to lose. She went to the window and looked out at the ocean that had nearly swallowed her. That it hadn't was a miracle, she supposed—or fate, or destiny, something like that, whatever you wanted to call it. "It's a blessing, really," she said. "The pregnancy wasn't viable. If it had continued, the fetus would have developed abnormally."

"Don't you think I know that?" Andrea said angrily. "I'm a doctor, for God's sake. I've said exactly those words to a hundred women, it doesn't make it any easier."

Kim couldn't find anything to say that would be both kind and true. Andrea had been so proud when she'd told their friends she was pregnant. There was nothing to be proud of now.

Play Nice, Be Good

Diana glanced out the window above the kitchen sink just as her sister Penny's battered SUV pulled into the driveway. Penny drove in her usual Mister Magoo style, leaning forward and squinting myopically; her two boys sat in the back seat. Pete, the elder, played with his phone while his little brother, Will, appeared to be jumping up and down.

"They're here!" she called out when Penny emerged from the car. As she rinsed her hands under the tap, Ted stampeded down the stairs and flew out the front door to greet his aunt and cousins. David came into the kitchen.

"Yippee," he said tonelessly.

Diana stood on her toes and kissed his cheek. "Don't be like that. It's only a few nights."

She wiped her hands on a dishtowel and went outside. She hugged her sister and bent to kiss her nephews, though Pete was almost her height now. He was a sullen-faced twelve, two years older than Diana's Ted. Will allowed himself to be momentarily embraced but refused Diana's kiss.

"He doesn't even let me kiss him," Penny said with an eye roll. "It's a phase he's going through." In Diana's opinion, something was wrong with Will, but Penny was oblivious, and Will, at four, was too young yet for school. Diana wasn't about to invite Penny's wrath by intimating Will was odd.

Penny opened the SUV's hatchback and dragged out a ratty tweed suitcase and a hard-sided carry-on wheelie.

"Come in out of this awful heat," Diana said. "It's wonderful to see you." She didn't say Penny looked wonderful. Her gray-brown hair was tangled and wild, and there were dusky bags beneath her dark eyes. She'd put on so much weight around her middle she looked as if she'd been pumped with air.

Inside the house, Diana poured Penny a glass of iced tea

from a pitcher in the refrigerator. "I guess you've already eaten," she said, looking at the oven clock. It was half past three.

"McDonalds," Penny said. "Big Macs all around."

Diana suppressed a grimace.

"Mom, can we go swimming?" Ted called from upstairs.

"Only if I'm watching," Diana called back. "Come on, let's go into the living room," she said to Penny. "We can see the pool from there. This heat wave is killer. Was it very hot in Virginia?"

"Pete is on the swim team at the Y," Penny said. "He doesn't need to be watched."

"What about Will?" Diana said.

"Pete's teaching Will how to swim."

"That's sweet," Diana said. "But Ted isn't old enough yet to swim without supervision."

"You ought to put him in a class at the Y," Penny said.

Diana cocked her head as if she were thinking, though she wasn't and didn't need to. "I don't know if we have a Y any-where around here." Belatedly, she realized she simply should have agreed. Ted went to a private day camp during the week. Will, she knew, was looked after by Penny's elderly neighbor when Penny was at work as a home health aide; it was a mystery what Pete did with himself all summer besides swimming at the Y.

"No, you wouldn't," Penny said.

"Wouldn't what?" Diana said evenly. "Have a Y here or know if there is one?"

"Both," Penny said. The three boys ran into the room before Diana could reply. Ted had on plaid swimming trunks; Pete wore cutoff jeans. "Where's your bathing suit?" Penny asked Will. He was wearing a pair of grayish-white BVDs.

"You left it at home, Mom," Pete said in an aggrieved voice. "It's not in either of the suitcases."

"Damn," Penny said. "Well, okay. We'll go to Target tomor-row." She looked at Diana. "If you *have* a Target around here."

"Of course we have a Target," Diana said. "This is Connecticut, Penny, not Oz."

"Connecticut," Penny said with disdain, sinking into the sofa cushions.

"Go on out, then," Diana said to the boys. She didn't like the idea of Will swimming in his underpants, and she felt sure he would pee in the pool, but there was nothing she could do about it. "Tell me your news, Pen. It's been ages since we've really talked."

"Not much to tell," Penny said. "Well, there's one thing. Bear is getting married." Bear was Penny's ex-husband. They'd been divorced just over a year.

"So soon?" Diana said. "Who is she?" She looked out the sliding glass door at Pete splashing water in Ted's face. Ted dove away from him. Will stood on the top step, staring at his half-submerged feet. She waited for Ted to explode through the surface before she gave Penny her full attention.

"Her name is Beth something," Penny said. "She's about twenty-five. I think he was having a thing with her while we were still married."

"Why do you think that?" Diana had never liked Bear. He and Penny had been high school sweethearts. Because he hadn't gone to college, Penny hadn't gone either. The last Diana heard, he worked in construction, but he changed jobs as if they were shirts, leaving Penny to bring in the steady money.

Penny shrugged. "Just a feeling. He started screwing around on me after Will was born."

"You never told me that," Diana said.

"Why would I?" Penny said. "You're conceited enough about your la-di-da life without me telling you my domestic woes." She stuck out her chin at Diana, daring her to shoot back.

Diana looked out at the pool again. Will hadn't moved from the top step. *Why must you insult me?* she felt like saying to Penny. Because she was here in Diana's house, comparing Diana's life to her own and coming up short on her end. Diana's law practice was thriving, and David made a good living in investments, but Diana believed that Penny would find reasons to resent her no matter what, because she had resented Diana since the day she was born, when Penny was three years old.

"You haven't been here thirty minutes," she said. "Can't we just have a nice time together, Penny? I've really been looking forward to seeing you."

Abruptly, Penny stood and went outside, leaving the sliding door open, hot air blasting in. Diana saw her fish a pack of cigarettes from the back pocket of her jeans. She put one in her mouth and lit it with a match, cupping the flame with her hand. The odor of cigarette smoke reminded Diana of their father, who'd died of a heart attack when the sisters were in their teens. Constantly, they'd vied for his attention, each wanting to be his favorite. When he died, they'd fought bitterly over who should have his wristwatch, exchanging increasingly poisonous insults, until their mother hid it away so neither of them could have it. Where was that wristwatch now? Diana wondered. Maybe Penny got it after all.

Ted swam over to the edge of the pool.

"Smoking is bad for you," Diana heard him say. "In school we learned that it's bad for all your organs, even your skin. Your skin is an organ, did you know that?" She cringed a little as Penny looked down at him; she knew that withering gaze. But Ted continued to watch her quizzically. After a few moments, Penny ground the cigarette into the grass with the heel of her flip-flop and wordlessly walked away.

"Where is she?" David said.

"You don't need to whisper," Diana said as she set the dining room table for six. "She's taking a nap. The boys are playing video games downstairs."

"Why do you put up with her?" he said.

"Why do you always ask me that?" Diana said. "Because she's my sister, I love her."

"She can be such a bitch to you." He ran his hand over his balding head and blew out a sigh. "It's like an urge she can't help indulging."

"Well, maybe it is, I don't know," Diana said. "Your sister is no treat either." David's sister was a history professor and a droning know-it-all; even David could barely abide her.

She went into the kitchen and opened the basement door. "Dinner," she called. Bleary-eyed, the boys stumped up the dim stairwell from the playroom below. Diana was surprised to see that Will was still wearing his underpants. "Pete, would you please take Will upstairs to change into some clothes? And will you tell your mother it's time for dinner?"

"He's okay the way he is," Pete said. "He doesn't really like clothes."

"What?" Ted said. "That's weird."

"Why don't you like clothes, Will?" Diana bent down and tried to catch Will's eye. He turned his face away. She realized she hadn't heard him speak a word other than "no" when she'd tried to kiss him earlier.

"He takes them off every chance he gets," Pete said.

Diana straightened up and put her hands on her hips. "Okay, but in this house we wear clothing to dinner, so please take him upstairs and put something on him. And you." She pointed at her son. "Go wash your hands and comb your hair."

When they'd gone, she mixed oil and vinegar and mustard and tossed it into a bowl of lettuce. David hovered aimlessly as she opened the oven door, took out a pan of baked ziti, and slid it onto the counter.

"There's something wrong with that child," she said in a low voice.

"He takes after Bear," David said.

"No, I mean really wrong."

"Like how?" He took a sharp knife out of a drawer and sliced the pasta into squares.

"I don't know." She put a finger to her lips. "Shh."

"Why are you shushing me?" David said.

She shook her head. "I'm shushing myself."

She took the salad to the dinner table. Penny came downstairs with Will, still wearing his grimy BVDs.

"*Another* phase he's going through," Penny said in a wry voice. "Getting him dressed is a major battle, and he's as strong as an ox. I'm just too tired to wrestle with him tonight. Do you mind?"

"Is he always like this?" Diana said despite herself. She couldn't stand it anymore. Will's face was as grimy as his underpants. His pale blue eyes appeared to be focused on something in the middle distance that only he could see.

Penny frowned. "Like what?"

"It's no problem at all," Diana said quickly. "He can wear whatever he wants."

"It's a phase, okay?" Penny persisted. "He's only four and a half. I doubt Ted is always easy."

"Not by a long shot," Diana said. "I hope everyone likes baked ziti."

Penny sat down at the table. Will climbed into a chair beside her. He *was* a bruiser, Diana thought, his arms and legs sturdy and muscled: he really did take after Bear.

"I thought we'd be eating outside," Penny said.

"In this heat?" Diana said. "Thank God for central air."

"I wouldn't know," Penny said—mildly enough, Diana thought. Penny ran her hand over Will's golden buzz cut. Dirty as he was, he had the face of a cherub. "We're used to hot weather, aren't we, doodle?" He gave no indication he'd heard.

David emerged from the kitchen with the pan of ziti just as the other boys came in. He served everyone from the head of the table, taking plates and passing them down. Diana looked around with satisfaction. The glasses and silverware sparkled in the evening sun; the summery floral cloth she bought last spring in St. Croix lay smooth and bright on the table. It made her happy to see Ted and Pete and Will playing and getting along. When they grew up, they would have each other, as she and Penny did.

"Will, do you like baked ziti?" David said.

"Oh, he eats everything," Penny said.

David grinned. "How about worms, Will? Do you eat worms?"

"'Nobody likes me, everybody hates me, I think I'll eat worms,'" Ted sang. He sat on the other side of Will. "Do you know that song, Will?"

"Don't do that," Pete said as Ted poked Will's upper arm.

"Why not?" Ted said, poking Will again. "I just asked if he knows the song. Do you, Will?" As Ted pointed his finger at Will's arm once more, Will raised his fork above his head and drove it into Ted's thigh.

"Oh, shit," Penny said before anyone could speak.

"I told you not to touch him," Pete said.

"Take it out, take it out," Ted shrieked. The fork stood straight up, as if Ted's flesh were a piece of meat. David pulled it out and covered the wound with his napkin, which was immediately soaked with blood.

"Hospital," David said as he picked Ted up in his arms and strode out of the room. Diana followed. Ted was still screaming as they left the house.

It was long past dark by the time they returned from the hospital, where they'd had to wait for ages to see a doctor. Ted's leg had gradually stopped bleeding, and cleaning and dressing the wound turned out to be all that had been necessary. Hollering in protest for being given a tetanus shot, Ted promptly fell asleep on the emergency room gurney.

"A four-year-old did this?" the doctor had said in disbelief. "He must have really meant business."

"Who knows what he meant," Diana had said, stroking Ted's hair. A blue-black bruise had begun to bloom around the line of puncture marks. Ted's blood was on her blouse.

When they got home, David took Ted upstairs and Diana went around the house, turning off lights she didn't remember turning on. Plates of food and the pan of ziti still sat on the dining room table, the tomato sauce congealed and lurid. Penny had gone ahead and eaten dinner without clearing up the mess. Outrage swelled in Diana's chest. As she cleared the table and washed the dishes, talking angrily to herself, she tried to think of something kind Penny had done or said in recent memory and came up with nothing. "Play nice, be good," she remembered their mother urging them when they were little girls. "Sisters are kind to each other." And she had always wanted to play nice with Penny. Now she wished she'd been as mean, even meaner, to Penny as Penny had been to her.

As she turned off the kitchen light and walked through the darkened living room, she noticed a pinhead of light through the window. She stopped and stared. It was the tip of a cigarette. Penny was sitting outside smoking. Diana went to the sliding glass door and violently pulled it open.

"What the hell, Penny?" It was a moonless night, and she could barely make out Penny's face. The air was suffocatingly humid, like breathing through a wet towel.

"What the hell, Diana." Penny was sitting on a deck chair that was usually by the pool. She'd pulled it out into the middle of the lawn and was ashing her cigarette onto the grass.

"Goddamn you," Diana said. She walked toward the moving ember. "You left that mess for me to clean up after all I've had to deal with tonight, while you sit out here giving yourself cancer. And you know what else? There is something seriously wrong with Will, and you are just too lazy or self-absorbed to notice it." Diana was nearly on top of her before she saw that Penny was crying.

"I know there is," Penny said.

Diana stopped. She hadn't seen Penny cry since they were little girls. Her eyelids appeared to be swollen, as if she'd been crying for a long while.

"Then why aren't you doing something about it?" Diana said.

"What am I supposed to do?" Penny said. "I don't have the time and I don't have the money to take him to one of those specialists. I work sixty hours a week, and now Bear isn't even contributing." She took a drag of her cigarette and ran the back of her hand under her nose. "The girl's knocked up."

"The girl Bear is marrying?" Diana could hardly believe how hot the night was; the temperature seemed not to have lowered at all from when Penny arrived that afternoon. As her vision adjusted to the darkness, she saw that her sister was wearing a tank top without a bra, her breasts lolling against her bloated stomach. "He has to give you money for the children, Penny, it's the law. You can take him to court."

"Time and money," Penny said wearily. "I can't miss work to go to court and I can't afford a lawyer."

"I'll give you money for Will," Diana said. "I'll pay for everything you need and help you get money out of Bear too. I'm a lawyer, Penny, you don't need to hire one."

Penny sat back and looked up at Diana. "Diana saves the day, eh? I'm a *lawyer*," she mocked. "You think you're so great."

Diana slapped her sister across her face. Penny sprang to her feet and tried to slap her back, but Diana had moved out of reach.

"I can't help it if you choose to be as trashy as you are," Diana said. "I went to school and worked damned hard to have what I have, and be who I am, and, yes, I *am* so great, a far sight better than you." She put a hand to her chest. Her heart was beating as fast as a bird's. She'd never said she was better than Penny before. "You think I feel superior to you? How could I not? You've been jealous of me all my life."

Penny stared at her for a long moment. She lit another cigarette off the final ember of the first and forcefully exhaled the smoke. Diana knew she'd landed a blow.

"Miss Homecoming Queen," Penny said. "You're as phony now as you were then. Your hair is dyed and your face is lifted, and you inject Botox or something into your lips that makes you look like a goddamn duck. Your kid is prissy, and your husband is pussy-whipped. And your house, Jesus, do you actually live here? I've never seen so many plumped-up pillows. You couldn't pay me to live in a town like this; it looks like Disney. So, you may think you're all that, but don't tell yourself I'm jealous because I'm not. I feel sorry for you, actually. You want so bad to be perfect, it's pathetic."

"I just offered you a lifeline for your child," Diana said. Her face and neck were slick with sweat, trickling into her ears through her hair.

"What you offered was me being beholden to you," Penny said.

"That's not what I was thinking," Diana said. "But forget it, the offer is off the table."

"I never considered it," Penny said.

"One of these days, Will is going to get into real trouble," Diana said. "Then you'll think back and wish you'd let me help him."

"Maybe. Maybe not," Penny said. She let a lungful of smoke drift out of her mouth and re-inhaled it through her nostrils. Diana turned and walked back to the house.

"Fuck you," she said before she went in.

"Fuck you too," Penny said almost cheerily.

Ted was so deeply asleep he didn't stir when Diana tucked him in. David was reading in bed. As she came into their bedroom, she suppressed the desire to fall into his lap and weep. Yet the sight of her sleeping son, her husband's studious face, the glow of the bedside lamp and her pillow ready for her head—these simple things steadied her and brought her back to herself. She went into her bathroom and rubbed a towel through her sweaty hair. Yes, she colored it, but so did most of the women she knew. She hadn't had a whole facelift; she'd only had her eyes done. She examined her face under the unforgiving overhead light. She went back into the bedroom.

"Do I look like a duck?" she asked David.

He frowned at her. "What?"

"And my hair. Do you like it blonde?"

David put down his book. "When are you going to realize that she is a complete bitch, Diana? She hurts your feelings nearly every time you speak to her."

She considered telling him about her argument with Penny, but he would only repeat what he'd just said. Anyway, maybe she didn't want to talk about it; she wasn't proud of how she'd behaved. She changed into her nightgown and got into bed. David turned out the light. She fell into a fitful doze, and then slept peacefully for a few hours, until she was woken by the sound of the toilet flushing across the hall. It was Penny, she thought, or Pete or Will; Ted had his own bathroom. When she checked her phone, she saw it was a quarter to one. A sound came from outside. She rose, went to the window and looked down at the pool.

"What are you doing?" David said, his voice complaining and muffled.

"Nothing. Go back to sleep," Diana said.

When David's breathing became regular and then rose to a snore, she went downstairs and out to the pool. The air had become drier; the stars were bright. The heat spell had finally broken. She pulled her nightgown over her head and let it drop to her feet. She walked down the steps into the water. It was black as tar and velvety against her skin, warmed by a week of unrelenting sun. She dipped beneath the surface and wet her face and hair.

"It's nice, isn't it?" Penny said. She was a ghost at the far end of the pool.

"Lovely," Diana said. She swam toward the deepest place where she could still stand on her toes. Penny swam around the edge. Water lapped against the tiles.

"Remember Daddy's watch?" Diana said.

"Sure do," Penny said. "What a squabble that was."

"I was thinking about it today," Diana said. "Whatever happened to it?"

Penny breaststroked toward Diana. "Don't you have it?"

"No. I thought you might," Diana said.

"I never saw it again," Penny said.

"It wasn't worth anything."

"I doubt it."

"It was worth the world to us then."

"I guess we've always been two cats in a bag," Penny said.

Diana floated on her back and listened to the sounds of the night, an insistent cricket and the hoot of an owl.

"I'd like it if you helped me with Will and Bear," Penny said.

"Of course," Diana said. "We'll straighten it out."

"I was a bitch to you about it."

"You're always a bitch to me, Penny. Why?"

"When I look at you, I see what I'm not. You know it and I know it; it's always been that way. You're a mirror I can't stand to look into."

"There's nothing I can do about that," Diana said. She wasn't going to feel sorry for Penny, or guilty either. She rolled over and stood up. Water streamed from her hair. "Will you be nicer to me please?"

"I'll try," Penny said. "But I can't make any guarantees. A lifetime habit of being bitchy...I'm just not that nice a person."

"That's not true. You're being nice right now."

Penny laughed. "Well, what do you know. And I'm not even trying." She went under and came back up, her face glowing like a pearl in the dark.

All Pies Look Delicious

Surely Emily Post or some other arbiter of good manners would object to bringing pie as a hostess gift, but Ella's friend Suzanne planned to do just that, and was very excited about it.

"I've never made a cherry pie before," she told Ella over the phone. "I pitted the cherries myself. It took all afternoon."

"How exhausting," Ella said. "But are you sure you want to carry it on the train tomorrow?" Suzanne and her husband Raoul were taking the train out to Connecticut from New York. It was a long way to have a pie on your lap, but Suzanne wouldn't be dissuaded. Ella thought it was presumptuous of her.

"Don't you agree?" she asked her husband after she hung up.

"I don't know," Neal said. "Big deal about the pie."

"I'm just nervous about Raoul."

"Relax," Neal said.

"You know I can't."

"Well, *try.*"

Ella sighed. Suzanne and Raoul came for a weekend every summer. Ella used to ask them for longer, but Raoul had been sinking into dementia for a few years, and his short-term memory was gone. Every other minute he asked, "How're you doing?" breathing over Ella's shoulder as she chopped vegetables or rinsed the dishes. At first, she felt compelled to vary her answers, thinking he would remember what she just said, until finally she understood that she could say, "I'm doing fine," every time he asked. He'd always been a sweetheart, but within the past year he'd begun to spit quiet yet startling obscenities. That there was never an obvious reason for it frightened Ella. She hoped he wasn't showing the tip of an angry iceberg. But Suzanne made him happy; she could coax a glimmer of intelligence into his eyes. Ella admired the grace with which her friend carried her burden. She wasn't at all sure she'd be as noble and kind if Neal were in Raoul's condition.

In the summertime, Ella and Neal lived in Ridgefield, Connecticut. The rest of the year, they lived in New York City, as did Raoul and Suzanne. The two women were very close, their husbands had always been friendly, though it was hard to tell if Raoul knew who Ella and Neal were anymore. When he wasn't repeatedly asking them how they were doing, he sat in a chair on the patio, seemingly content to gaze at the swimming pool, the occasional blue blossom from the surrounding hydrangea bushes swirling lazily into its filter. Suzanne lay next to him on a chaise, reading the odd item from the newspaper aloud as if he understood. "Fuck yourself," he might suddenly whisper. "You goddamn cunt."

"Please kill me if I ever get like that," Ella said to Neal the last time they saw Raoul. She couldn't imagine anything more terrible than gradually losing herself.

Suzanne was beautiful even at sixty-eight, tall and thin with salt and pepper hair styled in a dancer's high bun. She wore elegant flowing garments that she paid a seamstress to create out of silk, or chiffon, or gauzy linen in unusual colors that brought to mind the names of objects: eggplant, sea glass, sunflower, brick. Beneath these garments she wore leggings and flat sandals, affecting a bohemian glamour. Ella's summer uniform was khaki pants and long cotton tunics that disguised her considerable hips, and Spanish espadrilles in bright, solid colors that she bought online every year.

"You look fabulous as usual," she said as she and Suzanne hugged hello on Friday afternoon.

Suzanne was carrying a large purple shopping bag. "Ta da!" she said delightedly as she offered the bag to Ella.

"Oh, the *pie*." Ella took the bag and looked inside. The pie sat in a nest of bubble wrap, swathed in wrinkled foil. Neal came in with the luggage, followed closely by Raoul.

"Darling," Suzanne said. "Say hello to Ella."

"How're you doing?" Raoul said. He was a giant of a man,

with a razor-straight jawline and a prominent nose, hands as big as baseball gloves.

"Terrific, Raoul, how about you?"

"We're doing great," Suzanne said. "We have a girl now who comes in every afternoon. She and Raoul go for walks in the park." She looked at Raoul. "You love Sandra, don't you. We both do," she said to Ella.

"Let me put this in the kitchen," Ella said. "We can have the pie tomorrow night." Suzanne and Raoul followed her in. Already she was exhausted by Raoul's heavy presence. In a moment he would again ask her how she was doing again and the weekend would officially begin.

"Why not have it tonight?" Suzanne said as Ella slipped the pie into the refrigerator after removing its swaddling layers.

"I have strawberry shortcake planned," Ella said.

"Can't we have the shortcake tomorrow night? I'm dying to try the pie. Doesn't it look delicious?"

All pies look delicious, Ella wanted to say. Suzanne wasn't a gifted cook. "Good things come to those who wait," she said.

"Oh, that isn't true," Suzanne said. "I can't tell you how many things I've waited for that never arrived."

They ate dinner on the patio at a glass-topped table Ella found at an antiques fair. The table came with four black iron chairs that were artfully wrought with vines of ivy that stabbed the backs of whoever sat in them. In the middle of dinner Raoul stood up.

"Bitch," he hissed, and walked away to the pool. For a second Ella thought he was talking to her. She watched him stand on the edge of the coping and bow his head to the glowing reflection of the evening sky on the water.

"Raoul, sweetheart," Suzanne called. "Come back to the table."

"Do you want me to get him?" Neal said. He rose before Suzanne could answer and walked over to Raoul.

"You're so nice to have us for the weekend," Suzanne said. "I know Raoul isn't easy to be around, especially because of the cursing. It's gotten worse—well, he's gotten worse in general. He's forgotten how to dress himself, and now his appetite is enormous for some reason. He'd eat all day if I let him."

"I'm so sorry," Ella said. She wished Suzanne could leave Raoul at home; she longed to have her friend to herself. "But how are *you*?"

"Fine," Suzanne said.

"You never complain," Ella said.

"I've been very fortunate—" Suzanne began before an explosive splash made them both turn. Neal was in the pool.

"Neal!" Ella said. "What are you doing?"

"Fell in," he said. He ran his hand over his sopping hair and waded to the steps. Water poured from his clothes as he walked out of the pool, dragging on his polo shirt and jeans. He slipped his bare feet out of his ruined loafers. "I guess I shouldn't have had that second cocktail."

"You didn't have a second cocktail," Ella said.

"Then I guess I shouldn't have had the first!" He slopped across the patio to the house, blotting the gray flagstone with his footprints.

"How could that have happened?" Ella said.

"The light is fading," Suzanne said. "They were standing on the edge."

Ella put her napkin on the table. "Excuse me a minute, I'm going to see if he's all right."

Walking to the kitchen door, she caught sight of Neal through the open window of the laundry room, peeling off his clothes. She stopped and watched him. He would be seventy-two in August. The only pills he took were the occasional Viagra and a daily vitamin D, and he still played golf and tennis and mowed the lawn every week. She was the one with the sluggish thyroid, the arthritis and wrinkles and fat. But look at Raoul, she thought. Physically, he was robust, as handsome as ever. One could never tell by his appearance that his brain was full of holes.

She went into the laundry room and said, "What happened? Do you remember? Did you feel dizzy? Did you lose your balance?" She pursed her lips until they lost their color. "Tell me the truth, Neal."

Neal dumped the heap of wet clothes into the washing machine and wrapped a towel around his waist. "I didn't fall. Raoul pushed me in."

Ella opened her mouth and closed it. She put her palm to her cheek as if slapped. She stared at Neal for a moment. "What?"

"Shh, not so loud," Neal said. "My God, he's a strong son of a gun."

"But why?"

Neal shrugged. "Who knows?"

"Did he say anything?"

"Yes. He said 'cocksucker.' But I don't think he meant it personally. Or maybe he did. I didn't take it personally, anyway."

"I'm relieved on the one hand, but now I'm worried on the other. Is it not safe to have Raoul here? I'm going to talk to Suzanne about it." As she turned to go, Neal grabbed her arm. The combined scent of detergent and the chlorine from Neal's wet clothes was pungent in the closet-size room. Ella touched her nose with her wrist.

"No, listen," Neal said. "This weekend with us is the only break Suzanne gets all summer—all year, I bet. Do you think anyone else asks them to visit? Don't tell Suzanne. There's nothing she can do about it. It'll just upset her. I'll keep an eye on Raoul. Let Suzanne relax for a change."

"You are the sweetest man in the world, you know that?" She wrapped her arms around his damp, chilly body and kissed him on his lips. When they'd been together for eleven years, he had an affair with a woman he worked with, and then she retaliated by having her own affair with a caterer she'd hired for a party. She wanted children, but they couldn't conceive, and he refused to adopt. He was a skinflint. She was materialistic. He was dismissive. She was self-absorbed. It had been forty-six years of arguments, grudges, and complaints, but there had been, as well, many moments when each felt the other was perfect.

Suzanne's voice floated in on a breeze. "Don't do that,

darling, use your fork. Raoul, honey. Listen to me. Sweetheart, I said no."

Ella woke in the night to the sound of footsteps on the stairs. Blindly, she reached over to Neal's side of the bed and found his unmoving shoulder. The old floorboards on the first-floor landing squealed. She got up and put on an old cotton bathrobe and the espadrilles she'd been wearing earlier. She went to the top of the stairs.

"Who's that?" she called, hoping it was Suzanne. When no one answered, she went down the steps and stood at the bottom, listening. A crash of broken glass came from the living room. She crept in and turned on a light. A small framed print of an owl lay on floor, its protective glass scattered around it in countless glinting shards. Raoul stood over it, holding a brass fire tool with a hook at its end that was used to move burning logs. His crisp blue pajamas made him look like a huge naughty boy.

"Put that down this instant," Ella said sternly. She waited at a safe distance, afraid of what he might do, until he finally released his grasp and the tool dropped to the floor. The picture was a favorite of hers and she could see it was damaged. She went over and moved the tool back to its place by the hearth, then bent to pick up the print. She felt his big, warm hand flat on her back. "What?" she said, whirling around.

"Twat," he said. She looked into his eyes, as expressionless as a pair of marbles.

"Ella." Neal had come in behind her. He wore a T-shirt and boxers; his bandy legs were hairless on the lower part of his shins from the friction of decades of socks.

"He called me a t-w-a-t," she said primly. "And look at the owl, it's torn. Why is he suddenly being destructive? He didn't act like this last summer."

"Imagine what it's like for Suzanne," Neal said.

"I don't think he behaves this way when he's with her. She's never mentioned it. Do you think it's something about us, about being here?" She looked at Raoul, who was standing barefooted in the middle of the broken glass. Miraculously, his feet weren't cut.

Neil held out his hands. "Carefully, Raoul, take one big step toward me." Raoul stepped over the shards. Neil bent down and checked his feet, then led him out of the living room and up the stairs to his room. Ella was left with the ruined print in her hand.

She went to the kitchen, got a dustpan and broom, cleaned up the mess on the floor and dumped it into the garbage pail on top of the scraps from dinner. She looked at the oven clock: 4:32.

"So you're up too." Suzanne came into the kitchen. She wore an indigo printed Japanese kimono, its sash cinched tight around her waist. Her long hair fell down her back, a rippling gray and black river.

"I was thinking about what a lovely man Raoul was," Ella said.

"He was so much fun, wasn't he? Whenever I feel sad or sorry for myself, I remember all the good times we had. That's why we never had children, you know, we were too wrapped up in each other."

"No, I didn't know that," Ella said. They had never talked about why they didn't have children. For Ella, the subject was too painful, a Pandora's box of regret; she'd assumed the same was true of Suzanne and was surprised to hear otherwise. Sometimes Ella thought it was their childlessness that made them so *simpatico*; the subtle scrim of exclusion that existed between her and her friends who had children and grandchildren was nonexistent with Suzanne.

"Though lately I've been wishing we had," Suzanne said. "They would have been such a help now. What are you doing up?"

For a moment Ella considered telling her about Raoul. "Couldn't sleep."

"Raoul woke me up; he was wandering around the room. He was disoriented, I think, being away from home. I was knocked out from too much wine at dinner. Now he's sleeping like a baby, and here I am, wide awake and with a headache, no less." She sat down at the kitchen table and massaged her elbow. "Bursitis. Old age is a bitch."

"You're not even seventy," Ella said, sitting down. Their reflection in the black window startled her. "You're still gorgeous, you know that? I wish I had your looks."

Suzanne looked away from Ella. "I can't take care of him anymore. He's too much for me. He's gotten belligerent, and he's so big. I'm afraid of him sometimes."

Ella reached for her friend's hand. "Oh, Suzanne. What will you do?"

"I don't know." She squeezed Ella's hand and let it go.

"Why didn't you say anything about this before, Suzanne?"

"I'm ashamed, to be honest. I wanted to put on a good face for you, for everyone. It's pure vanity, that's all."

Ella began to cry. She was an ugly crier and knew it, so she hid her face with her hands. "I miss the way it used to be," she said. "The four of us."

"I do too," Suzanne said. "But those days are over."

"You're always so fucking brave about everything," Ella said furiously. She was never brave; it wasn't in her. She would have liked to be.

Suzanne smiled. "You sound like you hold it against me."

Ella sniffed and said, "Of course I don't," though she did just a little bit.

Suzanne asked Ella not to tell Neal about her trouble with Raoul, saying she wanted the weekend to be as "normal" as possible. Ella didn't see how normal had ever been possible with Raoul as part of the mix, but there was a garden tour that afternoon that she thought might be diverting. If Neal kept an eye on Raoul as he said he would, maybe she and Suzanne could get away for an hour or two. Suzanne hesitated—Raoul might become anxious without her—but in the end, she agreed with a sighing *okay* that Ella decided to read as relief.

The first garden on the tour was a maze of blossoming roses. The women strolled between faintly scented bushes thick with blooms in every shade; the path was glittering white gravel, impeccably raked, crunching discreetly beneath their feet. Ella knew the people who owned the house attached to the garden, or, more accurately, she knew of them.

"They're fantastically rich," she told Suzanne. "Pharmaceuticals, I hear." The house was gigantic compared to Ella and Neal's, a yellow clapboard colonial with added-on wings at both ends that were nearly as large as the original house.

"You've always been so impressed by wealth," Suzanne teased.

"Oh, everybody is, they just won't admit it," Ella said. She plucked a creamy bud. Gradually, she became aware of the army of bees hovering in and around the roses; their unrelenting buzz swelled in her ears. She didn't know what she'd been thinking, leaving Neal alone with Raoul. Raoul was twice Neal's size. She imagined her husband floating face down in the swimming pool, their house being devoured by flames.

Suzanne stopped walking. "I need to ask you a favor."

Ella was conscious of people stepping around them in the path. "Of course."

"I'll find a facility for Raoul to live in somehow—thank God there's money for that—but I need someone to take over his power of attorney should something happen to me. Would you and Neal be his guardians, Ella?"

"Of course," Ella said distractedly. Her heart hammered as she envisioned Raoul's giant fists making meat out of Neal's face. The kitchen knives were stored in plain sight on a magnetic strip attached to the wall. She stepped against a coral-blossomed bush and pulled Suzanne with her. "We are right in the middle of everyone's way here. Sorry," she said to a passing woman.

Suzanne looked around as if waking, her forehead creased in thought. "If I should die, Raoul won't have anyone."

"He'll have us," Ella said. "Please let's not think about death." Imagining having to visit an unresponsive Raoul in a nursing home made her inwardly cringe; she wondered how long demented people lived. She scratched her neck where she felt a tickle and was stung by a bee.

"Damn it!" she said. She clapped one hand against the sting and swatted the air with the other.

"Oh, ouch!" Suzanne said in sympathy. "Come on, let's get away from these roses."

They followed the path that led out of the garden and walked across a verdant lawn. The sky was pale blue and fading to white where it dropped beneath the trees; a diagonal bank of rippling clouds was moving in from the east. Anxiously, Ella strode ahead of Suzanne until they reached the car, parked bumper to bumper with scores of others along the sidewalk outside the house. A group of four girls were crossing the street. They were in their early teens, Ella guessed, all wearing flimsy little floral skirts that barely covered their behinds. She opened the car door and said, "Remember when we were that age?"

"We didn't know each other when we were that age," Suzanne said.

"I wish we had."

Suzanne chuckled. "Who knows if we would have gotten along? I was awfully fey in those days. I played the harp, if you can believe that. I had a boyfriend who fenced—you know, with a white jumpsuit and a phony sword."

"I probably would have had a crush on you," Ella said. "I didn't have a boyfriend until college, so I passionately admired the girls who did have them. I thought boys owned the path to glory. They actually do, if you think about it. Men are the gatekeepers, aren't they?"

"I suppose," Suzanne said. "I didn't mind. I don't mind. I'd rather take a back seat. Of course, that's not possible with Raoul anymore. He used to do everything for us; now I do everything for him."

Ella started the car and checked the rearview mirror, wondering how she would maneuver out of the tight parking spot. She backed up a few inches and turned the steering wheel, went forward a little, backed up once more, and turned the wheel again. "At this rate we'll be here forever," she said.

"One can hope," Suzanne replied.

Neal was slumped in a chair by the pool when Ella and Suzanne returned. His neck was turned at an angle so that his cheek was resting on his shoulder. His eyes were shut but his mouth was open; his legs were splayed like a jointless doll's. The paperback he'd been reading when Ella last saw him lay face up on the patio, and the bottle of beer he'd been drinking from was empty and overturned. Ella ran to him and pulled him up by his armpits with a strength she didn't know she had.

"Neal," she shouted. "*Neal.*"

"What?" Neal opened his eyes and shook her off. "Ella! What the hell are you doing?"

Ella sat down and massaged her biceps. "I thought you were dead."

Neal adjusted his shirt where she had ruched it up. "I was sleeping. I had a beer and that damn book was so boring. Why did you think I was dead?"

"I don't know. I was being silly." She touched the painful bee sting on her neck and decided not to complain. The sky was becoming overcast; they would have to eat dinner inside if it rained. She gazed unhappily at a congregation of drowned insects whirling around on the surface of the pool. She nearly told him about Suzanne's request, but realizing she was sitting where Raoul usually sat, she sprang up and said, "Where did he go?"

Neal shrugged. His casual manner was maddening. "He was here before I nodded off. Called the swimming pool a 'shit turd,' or I think that's what he said. Where's Suzanne?"

"She was right behind me. You were supposed to be watching him, Neal!"

"Don't shriek at me. They're probably inside."

Ella went into the house. The living room was empty; so were the dining room and den. She found them in the kitchen.

Raoul sat at the table eating Suzanne's pie. The crust was a jagged, glutinous ruin; pinkish-gray cherries oozed from it, deflated and bruised. He scooped his big hand into the plate like a shovel. Fruit and pastry fell to the table and floor as he crammed the pie into his mouth. Suzanne sat across from him. Her thin shoulders were hunched and shaking.

Ella called her name and went to her, caressed her wet cheek with the back of her hand. Raoul looked up and smiled at them. "How're you doing?" he said.

Talk to Me

Patched tin huts and cinder-block buildings lined an unpaved road so empty of traffic that dogs slept in potholes until the taxi driver startled them awake with his horn. Beatrice watched the animals skitter away down narrow, garbage-strewn alleyways, bone-thin and uniformly brown, as if they all came from the same litter. The frigid air that blew from a louvered vent raised the hairs on her arms. It had been shockingly hot at the airport: sweat had poured down her face as she and Peter waited for an hour at customs. Her left leg was two and a half inches shorter than her right, and though she wore special shoes to correct the disparity, it was difficult for her to stand for too long.

"I didn't know it would be like this," she said.

"Like what?" Peter said.

She gestured toward the window. "So poor." He wasn't paying attention, she knew. He lived in his head. But if she asked him what he was thinking about, he would say, "Oh, nothing much." Once, when she pressed him—*No, really, what?*—he gave her such a confounded look she never asked him again.

They had married the day before at the Glastonbury town hall with Peter's two brothers as witnesses. Conspicuously absent was Peter's daughter Joan, who had until recently been Beatrice's friend. Beatrice was fifty-three and never married, Peter was seventy-two and had been divorced from Joan's mother for over twenty years. Joan introduced them at her holiday cocktail party. "Would you mind talking to my father?" she'd asked Beatrice. Beatrice turned and saw a tall gray-haired man examining Joan's family photos on the fireplace mantle. "Why me?" she'd said. "Because you're my nicest friend," Joan replied in her disingenuously charming way. Days later she would say, "I asked you to *talk* to him, not *fuck* him," before hanging up the phone, though she'd seen them leaving the party together. She probably thought Peter was escorting Beatrice to her car. In fact, they took his car, a Mercedes sedan, to her apartment, where they made awkward but not unsatisfying love. His body was a long sack of drooping, spotted skin; she was frankly fat. She imagined his level of attraction to her was about the same as hers for him: in the upper range of mild, with periodic surges of primitive desire. At her age, sex was a rare brass ring, and she thought the same was true for Peter. She hadn't expected him to propose a month later, but she didn't say no when he did.

The taxi stopped outside a tall gate made of intricately woven palm fronds. As if by magic, the gate slowly swung in, revealing a courtyard paved with porous white stones and a high, open building roofed in the same woven pattern. A dark-skinned man efficiently checked them in; a young woman appeared out of nowhere and offered them flutes of juice on a tray. Then they and their luggage were driven on a golf cart through a jungle of cultivated plants: dwarf palms, banana trees, gaudy birds of paradise, and red and yellow hibiscus. Beatrice was grateful for the small breeze created by the movement of the cart because it was as hot here as it had been at the airport. But the air cooled considerably when they finally emerged from the jungle and pulled up by a bungalow adjacent to the beach. The ocean crashed and growled, spitting up geysers of foam; the sand was corrugated by the marks of rakes, all signs of seaweed removed. The bungalow was a white stucco box with a little porch that held a pair of rattan armchairs. Beatrice went inside. A plump duvet covered a vast bed, and the walls were as blue as the sky. She checked out the bathroom: two sinks in a sleek marble vanity, a marble bathtub, a glassed-in shower. She looked at herself in the mirror. Her lipstick was worn down to a ruddy edge that defined the shape of her lips, and there were black circles beneath her eyes where she had sweated off her mascara. With some difficulty she picked the wrapping off a little bar of soap and used it to wash her face. Tucking stray hairs into her unraveling chignon, she went back to the bedroom. Peter was already unpacking.

"What's the rush?" she said. She fell onto the bed; the duvet exhaled around her. A fan slowly rotated overhead, making a faint clicking sound.

"Looking for my bathing suit," Peter said. He pulled a pair of red swim trunks from his suitcase and began to unbutton his shirt. Beatrice sat up.

"You're going swimming?"

"Yes." He shrugged off his shirt and unbuckled his belt.

"In the ocean?"

"Where else?"

"There's a swimming pool. I saw it on the way to the bungalow." The pool was a large, perfectly round basin that had a palm tree growing from an island in its center. She planned to sunbathe tomorrow on one of the many chaises surrounding it, the scent of chlorine and sunblock reminding her of summer.

"I didn't pay for an ocean-side bungalow so I could swim in the pool," Peter said. "Come on, put on your suit. Join me."

Beatrice imagined trying and failing to negotiate the shoulder-high waves. She'd thought the ocean would be an undisturbed aquamarine plain like the pictures of Caribbean seas she'd seen on TV. "You go ahead," she said. "I'm tired." She wondered if she could sneak off for a dip in the pool.

"Call room service and order us a couple of drinks," Peter said. He put on his trunks and went out to the beach. She watched him dive beneath a wave; when she finally saw his gray head pop up, she realized she'd been counting the seconds. Joan told her father that Beatrice was marrying him for his money, but Beatrice's job as the head of alumnae affairs at a private college paid a respectable salary; she hadn't given much thought to Peter's wealth before his surprising proposal. "Does it upset you very much that Joan is angry?" she'd asked him during their brief engagement. Ruefully, he nodded. "But I know she'll come around. She can't stay angry forever. Does it upset you?" he asked. She said it did, but it didn't. Joan had a husband and a houseful of children; Beatrice had a parrot.

When Peter came out of the water, he and Beatrice showered and changed. Beatrice put on a yellow sleeveless sheath she'd brought specially to wear to dinner and wore her graying brown hair loose over her shoulders. The resort's dining room was somewhat dressy: Peter wore a light jacket. They sat on the porch drinking gin and tonics and watching the sky turn from pink to deep lavender to a nearly black blue. Though a thick sea grape hedge hid the bungalow next door, the voices of its inhabitants were faintly audible. A man and a woman—young, Beatrice imagined. She couldn't make out what they were saying.

"Maybe they're on their honeymoon too," she said.

Peter looked startled. "What?"

"The couple in the next bungalow. I wondered if they're on their honeymoon."

"I didn't realize anyone was there," he said. "Let's not make friends with them, do you mind?"

"I wasn't thinking we would," she said.

"Well, you're so friendly and attractive, people gravitate to you."

Beatrice laughed. She wasn't unattractive, but her skin bore the scars of adolescent acne. She didn't think of herself as particularly friendly—if anything, she was shy, self-conscious of her orthopedic shoes and uneven gait, even though she'd been told it was hardly noticeable.

"You don't need to flatter me," she said. He never had before. "Why don't you want to be friends with them? I'm not saying I want to, but I'm curious."

"I don't like meeting people on vacation, that's all. They're never the kind of people you would ordinarily want to know, and you end up having to have lunch with them, or they invite you to go deep-sea fishing, and then you're stuck with them for five days while they talk their heads off about their lives back in Peoria or wherever."

"How haughty you are!" Beatrice said with a laugh.

"I'm speaking from experience. Joan's mother made friends everywhere we went. Yak, yak, yak." He made a snapping gesture with his hand. "Everyone loved her."

"Except for you," Beatrice said.

"Well, obviously I loved her for a time."

"Did it ever occur to you that she might have been lonely?"

"Why would she be lonely?" he said.

"I bet you hardly talked to her."

He frowned and rattled the ice in his glass. "Why do you bet that?"

"Because you don't talk very much. For instance, we were sitting here for thirty minutes before you said a word, and that was only because I said something to you." Despite the breeze, the air was humid. She drew the back of her hand across her clammy forehead and said, "I'm not criticizing. It's just the way you are."

He didn't reply. The ocean sounded unusually loud. She had a meditation app on her phone that played recorded sounds from nature. The beach setting featured a rhythmic lapping and the distant calls of gulls.

"Are *you* lonely?" he finally said.

She thought of the decades of evenings she had spent alone at home, or gone to the movies by herself. True loneliness was a feeling she thought few people understood. It was a persistent pang that never eased, even in the company of others.

"That's a silly question to ask a newlywed," she teased.

"Of course it is," Peter said.

They ordered another round of drinks from room service, and then they went to the bar by the pool, where a young man and woman were huddled together, black silhouettes against the electric blue water. They murmured and nuzzled, then laughed aloud, playfully splashing each other. Beatrice watched them with amusement and envy. The few boyfriends she'd had when she was young cared more passionately about things like whales and apartheid than they ever had about her. She ordered a club soda and Peter drank a third gin and tonic. She had never seen him so tipsy. By the time they got to the dining room it was nearly nine, and only one other table was occupied. Peter ordered a bottle of wine.

"I'm unwinding," he said.

Beatrice smiled. "Unwinding from what, may I ask?"

"I haven't been married in twenty years, you know. It's an adjustment."

"I haven't ever been married," she said. She picked at her tuna steak. She didn't care for fish, but there had been nothing but fish on the menu. The dining room was a polished teak open deck with a high exposed-beam ceiling. Variously sized tables covered with white tablecloths were arranged at discreet distances from each other. Their table was near a miniature pond where every few minutes an invisible frog groaned.

"Why not?" Peter said.

"Why not what?"

"Why haven't you married before?"

She raised her eyebrows. He'd never asked her that. She hadn't asked him why he'd remained single, either. They were questions that bordered on rude, she thought, like asking a blind person why they couldn't see.

"Nobody ever asked me to," she said. She took a sip of water, tepid and faintly salty. Peter's silence felt like a condemnation, though his thoughts had probably moved on.

There was a group of four people a few tables away who spoke so loudly she could hear everything they said. They were late middle-aged, florid from the sun. The men wore polo shirts beneath their pastel jackets; the women had on bright sundresses that looked as if they were cut from the same pattern. They were reminiscing about another vacation they'd taken together, a cruise through the Panama Canal. One of the men had a squealing laugh that grated on Beatrice's ears.

"I wish to God they'd shut up," she said. Peter looked up from his dinner. His faded blue eyes were drowsy and unfocused. "Talk to me," she said. "Tell me something about yourself I don't know."

"I've been here before," he said. He spoke slowly and with apparent effort, his pronunciation slightly slurred.

"To Punta Cana?" she said.

"To this resort. A long time ago. With a friend."

She sat back. "Really? Why didn't you say so?"

"It was after I was divorced." Beatrice started to speak, but he continued as if he didn't hear her. "Joan's mother and I were married when we were kids, you see. I'd never been with anyone else. My friend was the son of a business associate. No one knew about us. It didn't last very long. I'm a coward; I was afraid people would find out."

"But you're not gay," Beatrice said. The skin above her upper lip began to perspire; she blotted it with her napkin. The frog groaned. Peter looked at the pond.

"Well. Not now. Not anymore," he said.

She stared at him. When they met at Joan's holiday party, he had immediately flirted with her, and though he'd been tentative when they'd had sex later on, she never imagined this was why. That his passion had waned since then seemed natural: she wasn't as passionate either after the initial thrill of having sex for the first time in years. He was nice-looking and kind and liked her. She hadn't needed more seduction than that.

"I thought you should know," he said. "Now that we're married."

"You might have told me before," she said loudly enough to turn the rowdy foursome's heads. A white-coated waiter came and took their plates away. She leaned forward and crossed her arms on the table. "Why did you ask me to marry you?"

He ran his hand over his face and blinked. "I've never had a steady relationship outside of my marriage. I've been basically alone for twenty years. The fact is I wanted a companion."

"Someone to take care of you." When he didn't answer, she said, "That's funny, because I thought the same thing, that you would take care of me."

"We can take care of each other." He reached across the table for her hand. She didn't let him take it.

"You've had too much to drink," she said. "*In vino veritas.* No, I'll tell you what you wanted. You wanted a nursemaid for when you get old and sick. I'm your insurance policy."

"I've never been sick in my life," he said. "If that's what you think, then why did you agree to marry me?"

"I wanted to be married. Is that so odd? Everyone I know is married. You've been alone since you were my age, but I've been alone my whole life." She tapped the tablecloth with her fingernail, leaving a crescent-shaped depression. "Please tell me why you brought me to *this* place, of all places?"

"Because I have happy memories of it. It's a beautiful place."

"It's not beautiful. It's just a fancy resort carved out of an impoverished island. It's as fake as Disneyland."

"I like you more than any other woman I've known," he said.

"Well, I gather there haven't been many."

He sighed. "I shouldn't have told you."

"I wish you hadn't." She looked at his hands resting on the table: brown spots, veins like worms, arthritic knuckles the size of grapes. She felt as if her life was bound by a series of stupidities that had led like links in a chain to this moment.

A waiter pushing a rattling dessert cart came abreast of their table. While he was explaining the selections, another waiter poured out the last of the wine. Peter ordered a cognac.

"Oh, why not," Beatrice said, and the waiter brought her one too. Peter raised his glass to the groaning frog. They drank in separate misery.

He was so drunk she had to help him undress. She pulled off his shirt as if he were a child, then poked him in the center of his naked chest and watched him free fall onto the bed. She went into the bathroom, confronted herself in the mirror, and was surprised to see that she looked the same as usual. She'd expected to look shocked and harrowed, visibly aged, new wrinkles etched into her face. She did look disheveled; she'd had too much to drink, though not nearly as much as Peter.

"Go ahead and divorce me if that's what you want," he'd said as she helped him to the bungalow. "I'm rich, you can have it all."

"Hush money," she said.

"Quiet," he mumbled. "Don't want Joanie to know."

"It's high time you came out of the closet," she said. "Nobody would give a damn. Gay marriage is legal for God's sake. You're a dinosaur, Peter. You're worse than a dinosaur."

"Well, you're better off than you were," he said.

"Oh yeah? How do you figure that?"

He stopped on the path and whispered loudly, "Somebody finally asked you."

She put on a short, satiny nightgown she'd bought with Peter in mind, took off her shoes, and went outside to the porch. Though the ocean had roared a few hours before, now it sizzled quietly, like meat on a grill. She limped across the beach and lay down in the powdery sand. The sky was black but for a white sliver of moon. She'd always assumed she hadn't married because of her leg. She had a few boyfriends when she was younger, but one by one they had peeled away and married other women. By the time she reached her mid-thirties, it seemed like there weren't any more men to date, and then she grew too old to have a baby, so there was no biological reason for her to exist. Now she would check the box that read "divorced" on official forms instead of the one that read "single." Maybe Peter was right: at least someone had asked her.

She fell into a fitful doze, and had short, disconnected dreams. Joan came to the resort and rented the bungalow next door; her mother, long dead, invited her to lunch, and presented her with a bridal bouquet. Her office mates had given her a little party the day before she married. Now she dreamt that a younger woman had taken her job while she was away. She squirmed insensibly in her sleep. A man who looked like Peter but wasn't Peter presented her with a shivering Chihuahua. *I already have a pet*, she said as her parrot flew out a window. She thought she was still dreaming when she was shaken awake by a boy.

"Are you okay?" he said. "I saw you from my bungalow and thought you were a dead body." Beatrice sat up. It was early dawn. The horizon was a brilliant orange stripe but the sky was iron gray. "I guess I watch too many crime shows," he went on. "Honestly, I was kind of excited."

Fine flour-white sand was in Beatrice's hair, glued to her legs and arms. She saw that the boy was in fact a very young woman, a gamine with pixie hair. "Was it you I saw swimming in the pool last night?"

"It was!" she said. "But then some guy kicked us out; we weren't supposed to be there so late. I'm Anne, I'm staying in that bungalow over there." She squatted down beside Beatrice. She was wearing running shoes and shorts and a man's grey T-shirt and smelled of bedclothes and sour breath. She reached into the pocket of her shorts and pulled out a joint. "Do you mind?" Beatrice shook her head. "That's a nice nightgown. I'm guessing you fell asleep by mistake." She lit the joint and offered it to Beatrice.

"I haven't smoked pot in ages," Beatrice said. She took the joint and inhaled deeply, holding the smoke in her lungs. When she exhaled, she said, "I can't believe I just did that. I mean, really, it's been thirty years at least."

"I like to get high in the morning," Anne said. "Before I take a run. So, what's your story?"

"My story? I don't have one," Beatrice said.

"I mean, who are you? Where are you from? All that." She handed the joint back to Beatrice.

"Oh. Beatrice. I'm from Connecticut."

"You're here with your family? Cool," she said. Beatrice decided not to contradict her. "I'm on my honeymoon. Been married three days."

"Congratulations," Beatrice said. All of a sudden, she was stoned. The horizon rushed forward and snapped back like a rubber band; she was filled with a deep satisfaction. "I'm really incredibly happy for you."

"Good stuff, eh?" Anne said. "It hits you harder if you haven't smoked in a while. I'm not sure I like being married. I thought it would make me feel like a different person, but I woke up the day after my wedding exactly the same as before."

"You know what?" Beatrice said. "I'm on my honeymoon too."

"Are you kidding me?" Anne said.

Beatrice shook her head and regretted it: a pain sliced across her crown. She took another toke from the joint. "I kid you not," she said.

"Do you feel different than before?" Anne said.

Beatrice thought about it. "Yes, but not in a good way."

"Why?" Anne said. "Never mind. None of my business."

"I'll tell you this much," Beatrice said. "You wouldn't believe how profoundly you can fuck up your life."

"Oh yeah, I believe it," Anne said. "I have already fucked up like a dozen times and I'm only twenty-four."

"At least you're married," Beatrice said.

Anne laughed at her. "So are you."

Beatrice imagined Anne's husband asleep in their bungalow, his hand resting possessively on her pillow. "You don't know how lucky you are."

Anne nodded. "That's what my mother says." She stubbed the joint out on the sole of her shoe and slid it back into her pocket. "I want to be back before breakfast arrives. We ordered it for nine, so I'm going to scram." She took off running down the beach, kicking up hunks of sand.

Beatrice sat like a doll with her legs spread in front of her, finding thoughts and losing them. The orange stripe paled as it bled into blue. Then the sky was a single color, cloudless and hard, and her shadow appeared on the sand.

"Jesus, it's hot," she said to herself. Her nightgown was sticking to her body. She stood up, dragged it over her head, and threw it to the ground. She strolled into the water and dove beneath a wave. The water was green as a bottle and murky, strings of seaweed floating untethered. A school of tiny grey fish darted past, then the same school, or perhaps another, darted past again. A conch shell lay half-obscured by sand, uninhabited and tragically cracked. Bubbles rose from her nose and mouth until there weren't any bubbles left. She broke through the surface and sucked in a long breath. Peter was standing on the beach, wearing his bathing trunks. His arms were crossed over his bare chest and his shoulders were hunched as if he felt cold.

"The thing is," she shouted at him, then forgot what she wanted to say. She swam toward the place that had been so beautiful at dawn. When she looked back, he was small.

Acknowledgments

Grateful acknowledgement is made to the publications in which these stories first appeared: "Identical" in *The Chicago Quarterly Review*, "Creamer's House" in *Folio*, "No Diving Allowed" in *Post Road*, "The Bottom of the Deep End" as "My Mother's Brother" in *The Valparaiso Fiction Review*, "Minor Thefts" in *Ploughshares*, "Attractive Nuisance" in *The Green Mountains Review*, "Dulaney Girls" in *Natural Bridge*, "Let Me Stay With You" in *Narrative*, "Pulling Toward Meanness" in *The Southampton Review*, "All Pies Look Delicious" in *The Briar Cliff Review*, "Talk to Me" in *The Pinch*.

Many thanks to my valued friends and readers for their unflagging support: Chris Cander, Lisa Cupolo, Joni Danaher, Katrina Denza, Kris Faatz, Sandi Fellman, Sharon Harrigan, Jill McCorkle, David Schweitzer, Douglas Silver, and my eagle-eyed first reader April Nauman. I am beyond grateful to everyone at the Sewanee Writers Conference and to the late Lee K. Abbott at the Kenyon Writer's Workshops. Jaynie Royal and Pam Van Dyk, thank you for this and for all you do.